MINDSCAPE TWO

LONE CASTLE
DOUBLED BISHOPS

OUTLANDERS OF THE MULTIVERSE
COLLECTION

BY D.N. LEO

Narrative Land Publishing
Narrativeland.com

PART ONE

LONE CASTLE

CHAPTER 1

Jennifer peeked into the children's chamber in the capsule where her grandson and granddaughter were being safely guarded. If she believed the information she had received, this was the best technology available in the cosmos to protect children outside the mother's body.

The children's room was sealed. All she could see were monitors displaying vital signs indicating the little ones were healthy. Heartbeats. Pulses. Biological and body formation processes.

Signs of precious life.

There wasn't a window in the room, so she opened the door of the chamber to look outside.

The Daimon Gate was an independent universe. Because of its special position in multiple dimensions, this universe was the gateway between member universes. Eudaiz and Earth were the two member universes she knew well and had a close affiliation with. She had been born and raised on Earth, and the rest of her family still lived there. Her sons, Ciaran and Tadgh, now held important positions in Eudaiz.

There were thousands and thousands of member universes that the Daimon Gate managed and protected. She didn't know them all. Members connected their gateways exclusively to the Daimon Gate. That meant citizens of these universes could only travel in and out of their universes and to and from other universes with the proper passes via the Daimon Gate.

The advantage of being a member was that trespassers and enemies could be prevented from entering a member universe because there was no other way to enter and exit unless one passed the Daimon Gate's strict scanning system—a wicked and unforgiving computer called the EYE. The more members the Daimon Gate had, the safer it was for them because members would protect the only gateway connecting the multiverse.

Safety for everyone.

Jennifer's husband, Conan LeBlanc, was the Host of the Daimon Gate—the highest position and equivalent to a kingship elsewhere. And that made Jennifer the Hostess. She didn't dwell much on the position and the perks that came with it. She loved her husband, and she wanted to be with him regardless.

A wave of compressed air blew past the field in front of her, loosening dirt and unearthing young trees. A stone at the gate flipped over and rolled down the hill.

It wasn't just wind. She knew it was more than that. But she didn't have the psychic ability to see minds like her daughter-in-law, Madeline. All she had was her gut instinct, and it was telling her that multiple entities were trespassing the gate right now. She couldn't see them. She didn't know what they wanted. She just knew they were present, and they wanted something she cared about.

The children.

Before she closed the chamber door, she saw Moira walking amid the gusts toward the capsule. Moira was her five-hundred-year-old ancestor, a formidable and powerful woman who had mastered several dimensions of the multiverse, earning herself a very long life. She had been speaking with Conan in the residence. Why was she now running back out into the wind?

Jennifer waited. Moira rushed in so fast she almost fell onto the floor. Jennifer slammed the door closed after her.

"They're coming for the children," Moira said.

"Yes. I guessed that. But what are we going to do? The children are in two gigantic boxes in a sealed room. I can't exactly scoop them up and run into the house with them."

Something smashed into the side of the chamber, which was no more than a mobile cabin without combat capability. Jennifer figured one more hit like that, and they would be rolling down the hill. "What the hell is that?" she asked.

"Haven't you been attacked before?" Moira asked.

"No. Not inside the Daimon Gate. For God's sake, if we're attacked *here*, there's nowhere in the multiverse that will be safe!" Jennifer exclaimed.

"That's a myth," Moira scoffed.

"A myth? Daimon Gate existed even before the concept of time. How can you say it's a myth?"

Another blow on the side of the chamber. It tilted. Moira darted toward the control panel and entered a series of commands. Jennifer heard humming noises from beneath them, and something snapped into place.

"We're now grounded," Moira explained, and she turned toward Jennifer. "I affixed permanent legs to the capsule. It will resist the wind and the attack outside. But I'm not sure how long it will last."

Something smashed against the chamber again. They heard the sound of claws scratching from right outside the door and walls.

"What's taking Conan so long?" Moira asked.

"What? You're not serious. He isn't leaving the residence, is he?" Jennifer asked but saw the answer on Moira's face. She rushed toward the door, but Moira snatched her away from it and swung her to the middle of the room. "If you open that door, you'll kill the children."

"If Conan makes it here, I'll have to open the door to let him in," Jennifer growled in response.

"Well, He'd better come with guards and an arsenal. At the moment, we have nothing to defend this birth chamber with," Moira snarled back.

"Why does everyone in the cosmos want the children? Yes, they're two of the best beings in existence, but so what?" Jennifer exclaimed.

"You yourself gave birth to a child of the Red Stage of the Daimon Gate. Look at how Ciaran has turned out. Look at the power he has. And now—there are twins. Of course, everyone wants them."

"Ciaran is my son. He will always be my child. I don't see any exceptional power or good it has brought him."

Moira laughed. "Don't be so sentimental . . ."

"Sentimental! You're not a mother. You'll never understand—"

An explosion cut Jennifer off. Its impact shook the chamber so severely she was afraid all the walls would cave in.

Then it went suddenly quiet.

An eerie quietness she didn't care for at all.

It was like the air and the life had been vacuumed from her surroundings. She scrambled to the door and pushed it open. The garden in front of her was a war zone. The bodies of guards littered the ground.

"Conan!" Jennifer whispered.

She charged out into the field of bodies, blood, and gore.

CHAPTER 2

Madeline gazed at the control panel and its jumble of buttons and symbols. She figured some of the buttons functioned in a way similar to the 'enter' key on her computer keyboard back on Earth. And she recognized a delete button—in her terms, the 'oops' button.

She was pretty sure the control panel operated by voice recognition. She should be able to just tell it what she wanted.

She glanced at the bed. Her husband still slept. It's not that he was a lazy sleepyhead—he was in something like a clinical state of mini-hibernation.

The battles they had engaged in before arriving in Eudaiz had drained all of his natural energy, so his body now operated on a temporary artificial energy that recharged itself every night during sleep. In this universe, energy was more vital than blood.

Madeline wanted to call her mother-in-law, Jennifer, in the Daimon Gate to check on her children. But it might not be a good idea. Although Daimon Gate should be the safest place in the cosmos to hide her children, the fewer people who knew where they were, the better it was.

Calling, or holocasting—similar to a call in Eudaiz—was a sure way to publicly announce their children's whereabouts. One of their executives was a mole, and there were invisible enemies out there who wanted Ciaran dead before his coronation. It was a given that their enemies would be hunting for every single opportunity to kill him, even if it included kidnapping his children.

She sighed and gave up the idea.

Ciaran stirred and opened his eyes.

She whooshed to the bed and pressed a kiss on his face. "Good morning, warrior! How are you feeling?" She smiled.

He rubbed his thumb across her dimple and pulled her down into his arms. "Why do you have to ask me that every morning? I'm not sick, Madeline."

"Let's just accept it as my ritual morning greeting until after your coronation when you won't have to wake up every morning not knowing how much energy you've got for the day!" She grinned. "And you know what? I'm your First Councillor now, a fully operating Sciphil One. And I am a lot stronger than you."

He laughed. "A Scientist Philosopher, you are! I see you've grown to love the term!"

She loved his laughter. "Hmm, not really. Let's stick with Sciphil. I'll pretend I don't know what the word means." She played with his long, raven-black hair and noted it had grown quite a bit in the last few weeks. It nearly touched his shoulders now, making him look even more like a warrior. *Her* warrior. "Gaia dropped by earlier to check on you," Madeline said.

"Check on me? She's only a child. She shouldn't be out and about by herself in the Sciphil zone."

Madeline shrugged. "She's one smart kid, let me tell you. She went from knowing a few basic English words to speaking just like you—overnight."

Ciaran pinched Madeline's chin lightly. "What do you mean by that?"

Madeline laughed and donned her best British accent, "Well, she speaks like this. It's a cheesecake. Dark, rich Belgium chocolate with a hint of chili and strawberries." She hoped he'd laugh again. His killer grins and the way his intense eyes twinkled and focused on her when he smiled never ceased to melt her. But instead, the smile faded from Ciaran's face.

Madeline was puzzled. "I did my best with the accent. Guess I need more practice. What's wrong, Ciaran?"

"That was the dessert we had after our first dinner together in London. That was my description. You remember it."

She didn't tell him she remembered the very first moment they had collided in Hyde Park. She remembered everything—what he wore, the way he looked and spoke, and even the smell of his perspiration.

"You remember that fine detail of our first date," Ciaran repeated.

Madeline arched an eyebrow. "Yes, I have a good memory. Why is that a big deal?"

Ciaran shook his head and sat up. "Sometimes it's better to just forget," he mumbled and headed toward the bathroom.

An image flashed in her mind. Her psychic ability switched on, and she saw Ciaran's mind. It was rare for her to see it out of the blue. And especially when nothing significant was happening. Or *was* there something significant happening?

"We've come up with the name Caedmon for our son. But we don't have a girl's name yet, Ciaran. How about Lyla?"

That was the word she had just seen in his mind. He turned around slowly. The look on his face made her want to recoil. But she didn't. She manufactured a smile. "What do you think?"

"Anything but Lyla."

His voice was so low, it came out more like a hiss.

"But I like that name. If you don't, can you tell me why?"

He shook his head and strode out of the room.

"Don't walk away from me, Ciaran." She raised her voice. "There can't be secrets between us. Not back on Earth. And especially not here . . . not . . ." It might have been her tone, what she said, or the fact the she started to breathe heavily as if she was in shock that stopped Ciaran in his tracks.

The precognition hit her liked a tidal wave. In front of her was a flash of images.

Blood.

Zombies.

Snakes.

Space creatures.

And Conan—Ciaran's father—covered in blood. In her vision, she pushed the monsters away to save Conan. But there were so many of them. Without a weapon, she couldn't do much.

She pushed and shoved, but it had no effect on the monsters.

She cried.

And then she was floating. Ciaran was shaking her. She opened her eyes and found herself in his arms, and she saw the terror on his face. The thin material of his sleeping shirt had been torn. She saw trails of blood on his chest where she had scratched him.

He wiped the tears from her face. "I'm sorry. Don't cry. Let me take you to bed."

He carried her to bed and wrapped her up in a blanket. Her teeth chattered uncontrollably, and she couldn't even speak. He climbed onto the bed and held her tightly. She could feel his muscles quivering as much as her own. She could feel the vibration of his anxiety. She knew he suffered from her vision as much as she did even though he didn't have any psychic abilities and hadn't seen what she'd seen.

After a while, her temperature evened out. Ciaran looked at her and asked, "I guess this was one of your psychic episodes?"

She nodded.

"If it's this bad, then we have to do something about it," he said.

"I saw—"

He locked her lips with a deep kiss to cut her off. When he finished, he said, "Whatever terrible thing you saw, we'll fix it. Okay? I want you to know that."

She nodded again. Before she could say anything further, a robotic announcement broadcast from the speaker.

"You have a holocast from Jennifer LeBlanc."

"Accept," Ciaran said.

"Affirmative," the robot said.

Then Jennifer's voice came across, "Ciaran, your father's in trouble. Come at once."

CHAPTER 3

Everyone called him Master. He liked it. Creatures in space, humans on Earth, and paranormal creatures feared him, at least those he was in contact with. He had never told them his name, so he was happy their fear translated into the name Master.

He was the master of many things. But sorcery was his forte.

It had been hundreds of years that he had walked the cosmos, living in multiple dimensions and multiple universes. He had no place he could call home, but there was one place he wanted—Eudaiz.

Among the many things he couldn't have, Eudaiz had always been his most desirable goal and the most painful failure he had ever experienced in his very long and unnatural life.

Unlike the many pathetic creatures he hired, he would never give up. One day, he *would* take his rightful place in Eudaiz, and he was willing to do whatever it took to get there. He had sacrificed enough. There had always been one hurdle between him and Eudaiz—the LeBlancs. But he'd learned his lesson. This time, he would be successful.

He would be where he deserved to be.

He wiped the gore of Kyle's body, a remnant of the explosion, from his hands. "You're useless," he muttered. The tasks he had given Kyle were simple—capture the children and replace Sciphil Seven.

Kyle had failed both jobs.

Now he would have to get his hands dirty and handle some trivial matters.

He shook his head.

There had been too many errors, and the coronation date had crept up faster than he wanted.

There were too many things to do and not enough reliable creatures in the multiverse to hire.

He turned on his communication channel, blocked the visual, and called his spy in Eudaiz. "Give me some good news," he said.

***

As soon as the capsule landed and he verified his palm print on the control panel, Ciaran strode straight to the gate of his parents' residence in the Daimon Gate. Madeline was right beside him. She always was. And he would need all of her support very soon.

The grand reception room reeked of the stench of blood. The bodies of guards were everywhere. Blood smears painted the room. On the shiny white floor. On the polished marble benches. On the white walls decorated with classical paintings. And on the glass of the windows.

Jennifer stormed in from the hallway. Ciaran rushed over to hold his mother. He knew she would never allow any sign of weakness to show. But at the moment, fear had taken over his mother. She was incoherent. So he did what a son should do. He comforted her.

Ciaran signaled Madeline. She came to stand next to Jennifer. Ciaran turned on the control panel to check the computer system. The computer didn't detect the carnage. It thought everything was operating normally, and that Conan was most likely relaxing in the room, drinking his tea.

"Do you sense any Black Rock creatures here, Madeline?" Ciaran asked.

"No," she answered.

"The computer detects nothing," he muttered.

"It was a tremendous explosion. The gusts from it almost blew your children's chamber away. How can the computer see *nothing?*" Jennifer exclaimed.

"The attackers were invisible to the system. The EYE is the most sophisticated computer system in the cosmos. If it can't detect the creatures, your gate security has no hope."

Jennifer flopped down heavily in a chair. "It was my fault," she cried. "I was always thinking of Eudaiz. If things went wrong, it had something to do with Eudaiz. If someone attacked us, it was because of Eudaiz. There are nine thousand gates within the Daimon Gate, and each one is connected to thousands of universes. But I've never thought much about them. I left the residence defenseless and locked myself in the children's birth chamber because I thought that was what they had come for."

Ciaran crouched next to his mother and held her hands. "You're not thinking straight, Mother. Eudaiz is the most prosperous universe. Of course it's the most likely target for attack. Go easy on yourself."

"If they targeted Eudaiz, they must be the Black Rock, right? Can you go there and bring your father back? You've been there before to rescue Tadgh."

"Madeline didn't sense any Black Rock creatures in here."

"But if it wasn't them, then who else?" Then Jennifer looked behind Ciaran. "Where's your brother? Why isn't Tadgh with you?"

"Mother, Tadgh has just taken his Sciphil Seven position. He's still in training. I didn't tell him anything yet."

"Your father is missing, and you didn't think to tell your brother? I know Conan isn't your real father, but he brought you up, and he's the only father you know."

He knew his mother wasn't thinking straight. But he didn't expect what she was saying would hurt him so much. "Mother, you're being unreasonable."

21

Madeline pushed her way in and held his mother's shoulders so she looked straight into Madeline's eyes. She said, "You know I have psychic ability. I told you it wasn't Black Rock creatures. If you insist that Ciaran go to Black Rock, it will be a waste of time and effort."

Ciaran turned away from his mother. He looked out to the garden where he had parked the birth chamber of their children, and his blood ran cold. His mother had left Moira, his wicked ancestor with a vested interest in the children, alone in the birth chamber.

Saying nothing, Ciaran darted out of the house toward the chamber.

***

Moira turned around and smiled at Ciaran when he stormed into the room. In the confined space, he could feel the vibration of her energy. Her formidability and authority would have overwhelmed any creature in the cosmos.

"You were afraid I'd take your children, Ciaran?"

"I trust no one when it comes them."

"Well, you don't have much of a choice, do you? You can't take soldiers into the Daimon Gate. Now that your father's been taken, will you go and rescue him, or stay here and guard your children . . . against me? We have an agreement, Ciaran. If you hold up your end, I will mine. Your mother isn't thinking straight right now. But you are the king-to-be of Eudaiz. You cannot let your judgment be clouded by such trivial matters."

"My father is missing. That's not trivial. Not to me personally, and not to the Daimon Gate and the safety of the cosmos. If he is held for ransom, it will be catastrophic."

"Not really," Moira said matter-of-factly. "If Conan is held against the interest of the cosmos, he will kill himself. That's just a necessary responsibility of a man in his position."

Ciaran punched the wall so hard it shook loose a wooden panel.

Moira continued, "Human emotion is your weakness, Ciaran. You have to get it under control, or you'll be in serious trouble."

"I know what I'm capable of. I don't need your advice," Ciaran snarled as Madeline and Jennifer stormed in.

"How is quarreling going to help the situation?" Jennifer raised her voice.

"He's upset because you weren't thinking straight. Don't blame that on me, Jennifer," Moira said.

Jennifer sighed. "I'm sorry. I didn't mean what I said about . . . Conan."

Ciaran turned around and looked at his mother. "He's the father I've known my whole life. And he will always be my father. But he didn't give me my life—"

"I know, and I said I'm sorry, Ciaran," Jennifer cut in.

Ciaran nodded. Moira was right. He was too emotional about this. He was glad his mother had cut in. Otherwise, he could easily have ranted on and on about the fact that he'd had to kill Bran, his real father, for Conan. He didn't regret it. He had done what he had to do. But he would never forgive himself for doing it.

Madeline walked toward the two boxes that contained her twins. She traced her hands across the glass panel. Ciaran approached from behind. He removed her hands and held them in his. "Our children will be fine, Madeline."

"I'll look after them when you leave to rescue Conan," Moira said. "How many guards do you have left, Jennifer?"

Jennifer shook her head. "We don't have any residential guards left alive. But we have hundreds of thousands of guards at the gate at our disposal. All I have to do is to call the committee."

"Don't," Ciaran said. "If you call the Daimon Gate committee and tell them their leader is missing, you'll spread confusion and fear. That's a recipe for chaos and will lead to disastrous consequences. It might be exactly what Father's kidnapper wants."

"Welcome back, Ciaran," Moira smiled. "Precisely. The Daimon Gate is the only secure gateway to the multiverse for thousands of universes. If an outside universe wants to invade those member universes of the Daimon Gate, they will need the Daimon Gate to be vulnerable. Chaos is the best strategy to weaken it. And capturing Conan is a good way to create chaos—*if* we give in to what they want."

"I've been to the Black Rock. I've seen their creatures. They don't have the capacity to pull this off," Ciaran said.

Moira shook her head. "It's not the Black Rock. It's far worse."

CHAPTER 4

Sizx hunched over the control panel in her workstation. There had been some issues with the data migration all morning. She could fix it, but data manipulation wasn't her strength. She was best in spy devices.

The problem wasn't severe, but she had been distracted. She couldn't get the memory of the night's encounter with Ciaran out of her mind. She was the head of intelligence of Eudaiz, a position that was so important she couldn't afford to have any weaknesses.

Emotion was a weakness.

Humans suffered it most.

She wasn't human. She was a Eudaizian. And she should be able to control her desire and urges for a man. She sighed, it was Ciaran she was thinking about. Not just any man.

Maybe she should court a male counterpart in the Eudaizian community. There were billions of them out there. And she wasn't exactly lacking in looks. She should have no problem finding a man.

Ayana whirled into the room so fast it startled Sizx. They always communicated using holocasts. Ayana had never set foot in her station before. She was Sciphil Two, the second in charge after Ciaran. What brought her here must be a universe-shattering matter.

Without a greeting, Ayana shot right to the point. "I didn't want the holocast recorded. That's why I'm here. Can you locate Ciaran's capsule for me?"

"Yes, ma'am," Sizx muttered and concentrated on the task. Ciaran's capsule wasn't on the radar. It was as if it had vanished.

"Can you message his wrist unit via private channel? The central computer wouldn't have access to that?" Sizx asked.

Ayana shook her head. "I tried. He didn't respond." She whirled around the room, walking back and forth. "He's got to understand how important this is," she said.

"Is there anything else I can help you with?"

Her question jolted Ayana back to reality. She was at Sizx's station, not in her own office. Ayana paused for a moment then shook her head. "No. There's nothing you can help with unless you have another way to locate Ciaran's whereabouts."

"No, ma'am."

Ayana nodded. "Okay then." And she turned on her heel.

"How important is it?"

Ayana stopped in her tracks. "How important is what?"

"The matter that you have at hand? The reason you have to locate Ciaran's whereabouts?"

"Eudaiz's safety is at stake. It's very important. Ciaran is new to all this. He wouldn't understand the scope of the problem. I need to talk to him."

Sizx nodded. She drew in a breath and said, "I might have a way to track him."

Ayana arched an eyebrow. "Oh really?"

***

"Are you sure? That place doesn't look like it even exists!" Jennifer exclaimed, staring at the search results Ciaran had just pulled up on the computer screen.

Standing in a corner of the computer room, Moira waited patiently.

Ciaran turned around to look at Moira. "Xiilok doesn't exist anywhere. That's why creatures from there cannot be detected. But how do you know about it?"

Moira smiled. "As I said, I'm not going to tell you how I know. But Xiilok is the only place that could produce this sort of soldier. You can choose not to believe me—"

"I do. I believe you. Please tell us about Xiilok," Jennifer cut in.

Moira nodded. "Xiilok is the opposite of the Daimon Gate. While Daimon Gate is the connection between participating universes, and it validates legitimate passengers, Xiilok is the place for multiversal outlaws. Xiilok fighters don't have forms that carry energy. They retain the physical form they had before being turned into a Xiilok. When they die, they disintegrate into black puddles

30

filled with swimming worms. Because they don't have live energy, computers cannot detect them. They can slither straight into the Daimon Gate completely unseen."

Jennifer teared up. "You're saying they're *invincible?* What do they want from Conan?"

Moira shook her head. "Xiilok is neutral. It doesn't have a leader, a government, or a policy against any universe. Xiilok fighters are freelancers who fight and kill for a living."

Ciaran's blood ran cold. "It's not the Xiilok that want Father. It's someone else. Someone who knows the multiverse well and knows how to use illegal forces that are undetectable. And capturing Father would create chaos inside the Daimon Gate. I can only think of one plausible motive for this— invasion of a member universe."

Moira nodded. "Yes, the Daimon Gate is the only gateway through which they can bring a massive amount of soldiers into the member universes."

Jennifer said nothing more. Tears rolled down her face. Ciaran approached and held his mother's shoulders. He looked into her eyes. "I will go to Xiilok and bring him back. I want you to trust me and wait for me. Don't do anything drastic. Don't call your committee yet. Can you do that?"

Jennifer nodded. "Be safe."

"I'll go with you, Ciaran. That's the word of your First Councillor, not your wife," Madeline said.

"Shouldn't we send troops with you two to Xiilok? You can't go to a strange universe on your own," Jennifer said.

"You can't take ordinary troops into Xiilok. It's a universe of illusion. You'll send your troops to their death. But Ciaran and Madeline can survive as individuals if they fight their way through it. In Xiilok, nobody cares about anyone else's business. They work for money. It's the land of multiversal outlaws. They have been rejected by the entire multiverse, and the only thing they care about is currency. You pay them, they'll work for you. It is as simple as that," Moira said.

Ciaran smiled. "Fortunately, wheeling and dealing is one of my specialties. There is no need for super troops."

"But I'm sure some super soldiers would help," Madeline said.

"Unfortunately, we are not at a stage where we can create super soldiers yet. Not for a long while," Ciaran replied.

"I have some psychic ability, and I can guess direction. But if Xiilok is that mysterious, I'm not sure my psychic ability will work. Do you know how to get there, given that they're not on the map anywhere?" Madeline asked Moira.

"I have never accessed them via the Daimon Gate. But there *is* a system where you can find information about anything in the cosmos, including the entrance to Xiilok." Moira donned a wicked smile.

"If the EYE is what you're thinking about, I don't have access," Jennifer said.

The EYE was the most advanced computer surveillance system in the cosmos. It recorded everything in the cosmos and was managed by the Host of the Daimon Gate. An attempt to breach the EYE databank would bring a death penalty to any unauthorized individuals.

Moira laughed. "I can see Conan embraces the ethics of his position. Even his wife doesn't have access to the databank."

"You know very well the EYE is not just a databank," Ciaran said. "It stores the history of everything in the multiverse. Anyone with access to that much data will have the power of God." Then he turned toward his mother. "Still, I need to access the EYE, Mother."

"You're not hacking it. I won't risk your life for this. Your father won't, either," Jennifer exclaimed.

Ciaran smiled. This ordeal had seriously knocked the wits out of his mother. "I didn't say I'll *hack* the EYE. But every computer system needs maintenance. Where is it done, and who handles it?"

Jennifer's eyes lit up. "Oh, for sure. Computer maintenance, that is. I know just the person for that. You father recruited a geek from London to upgrade the security for the system. Before upgrading, he needed to do an audit first. I'd imagine that guy would have the access you need. And this was a side project. Your father didn't report it to the committee."

Ciaran arched an eyebrow and smiled. He said nothing. Jennifer tossed him an electronic pad. "Here's the map. The address is installed in there. His name is Lorcan Brody."

CHAPTER 5

Daimon Gate was an ever-changing universe. That was why trespassers tended to get lost and drop to the bottomless oblivion. Ciaran and Madeline faced a strange landscape. Rolling, green hills reached to the horizon and were topped by a twelve-shade rainbow. There were no forests, mountains, rivers, or anything they had been familiar with on Earth.

Suddenly, everything changed color. The rainbow vanished. The hills shifted aside, and forests grew on their left and a raging river appeared on their right.

"I'm afraid this change confused my sense of direction," Madeline said.

Ciaran chuckled and look at the electronic map his mother had given him. An indicator for direction appeared and pointed to the west. "Let's go," Ciaran said.

"That's a canyon. Are we supposed to climb down?" Madeline exclaimed in fear.

Ciaran laughed. "I'll bet it turns into something friendlier when we approach."

Indeed, when they came close, the gigantic canyon shrank down into a road flanked by wild roses.

"So this is the reason they can't build any fixed transportation system in here," Ciaran said.

"All I want is to be sure that when I set my foot down, whatever is beneath it turns into solid ground. We haven't yet developed the ability to fly," Madeline said.

There was no linear dimension in the gate. They walked a few steps and passed through a dimensional gate to an area with a totally different setting. One minute, there was an endless snow field, and the next, a desert.

Madeline totally lost her perspective of time and space.

With the guidance of the device Jennifer had given them, they soon found Orla castle, looking down at them from the top of a hill. Ciaran led the way to what looked like the main entrance. There was no guard and no security. The property seemed more residential than castle-like. Before Ciaran could push the doorbell, objects began to rain down on them from the open window above—picture frames, clothes, shoes, a suitcase, cosmetics, glassware. Ciaran pulled Madeline under the cover of the entrance to prevent her from being hit by the household items.

A woman's voice shrieked, "See if you can live without those things!"

"Looks like Lorcan's wife is a thrower and a shrieker," Madeline chuckled.

Ciaran rang the doorbell. A male voice snarled harshly from a speaker, "What?"

"I have a message for you from the Host," Ciaran said.

"Huh?"

"The Host has a private message for you, Lorcan Brody."

The voice rumbled, and in a moment, they heard footsteps, and the door slid open to reveal the speaker himself—tall and slender, masculine face, ruffled black hair, striking blue eyes, and gorgeous lips. His unbuckled belt dangled from his jeans, and his shirt was unbuttoned, revealing toned abdominal muscles made for sex. Madeline cleared her throat and couldn't conceal a smile.

Lorcan stared at Madeline and Ciaran. He slammed the door closed and then opened it again.

Madeline chuckled. "We're real."

Lorcan cleared his throat. "Ciaran LeBlanc and Madeline Roux."

"Have we met?" Ciaran asked.

"Yes. No. Excuse me." Lorcan buttoned his shirt and tucked it into his jeans and fastened his belt. "We're having a little domestic problem. Excuse me." He rushed outside, slipping his feet into a pair of shoes lying on the ground.

"For a moment, I thought you guys were going a little wild." Madeline smiled at him.

Lorcan grinned. "More often than not, we . . ." And then he saw the look on Ciaran's face and put his grin away. "What does the Host require of me? He said he wouldn't give me a new job until I finished the current one." Lorcan invited everyone inside and led the way to a hall.

"How do you recognize Madeline and me?" Ciaran asked.

"When I was on a job in London, I saw the both of you. It's a long story."

"What sort of job?" Ciaran asked.

"Let's just say I extract information from computer databases when a client requests."

"You're a data thief. A hacker." Ciaran chuckled. "And your position here is to handle computer security!" Ciaran admired his father's flexibility in this matter. While he wouldn't give his mother access to the databank, he had hired an ex-thief to handle security.

"Apparently, I'm the best man for the job. Ciaran, London is in the past. I'm happy here. My wife and I can build a good life here. I'm good at what I do, or the Host wouldn't have offered me the position. What can I do for you?"

"I need access to the system," Ciaran said.

"Look, I know you're a big fish in London. But here, I work for the Daimon Gate and will only answer to the Host. I appreciate the opportunity to live here and will never do anything to jeopardize it. Now if you don't have a message from the Host that I can verify, I'm afraid you're no longer welcome here. I'm no fighter or guard, but no machine here will work for you if you're not eligible to gain access."

"Give me a verificator," Ciaran said. Lorcan nodded and fetched a small device, giving it to Ciaran. Ciaran pressed his left palm on it.

"You're left-handed. My wife, Orla, she's left-handed too," Lorcan said.

Madeline glanced at Ciaran and smiled. They said nothing to clarify the fact that because Ciaran was the king-to-be of Eudaiz, his verification data was stored on the left and not the right palm. As Lorcan didn't appear to know much about it, it worked in their favor.

The machine identified Ciaran as the king of Eudaiz and gave him full access. Lorcan looked at his device, shocked. "Full access? You've got to be kidding me." He turned the machine off and on and gave it to Ciaran again. Ciaran patiently verified himself again. The device displayed the same information.

Lorcan shrugged. "This little machine doesn't lie. I don't care which country you're the king of, if it verifies you and confirms that you have full access to my system, then you'll get it. A note of warning— my system is quite sophisticated. It's not a databank—it's a real machine. Do you need help operating it?"

Ciaran smiled. "No, I'll manage." Lorcan led them to the computer room, verified, and turned the machine on.

"I really don't want you looking over my shoulders as I work. I understand that your machine is your territory, but I really do need to work on it by myself," Ciaran stated. Lorcan mumbled his protest and left the room.

Ciaran hunched over the machine, his fingers flying over the keyboard. He shook his head. "This is taking too long. Could you please call Lorcan in again, Madeline?"

She fetched the former hacker, who had been lurking outside the room. He didn't need a second invitation. Once inside, he arched an eyebrow as he saw the progress Ciaran had made with his machine.

"You'd make a good data thief. But you still need me." Lorcan smiled.

"No, I don't need you. I need time that we don't have. You shouldn't need five pass codes for every single command. I can crack all of your codes, but I don't want to waste my time doing that," Ciaran remarked. "Could you please run the search command on entry and exit incidents by creatures without traveling permits? I need to know where the incidents occurred. Use the data in the EYE."

Lorcan narrowed his eyes. "I don't have access to the EYE."

"Don't test my patience. You saw I have full access to the data," Ciaran snarled.

"Yes, the ordinary data, and even my data, but not the EYE."

Ciaran pulled his dagger and pressed it into Lorcan's throat. He lost his cool thinking of his missing father, the uncertainty of Eudaiz's future, and his children waiting for him to return. "I'll see how loyal you are to a machine."

A small stream of blood dripped down Lorcan's throat from where the tip of the dagger pressed into his flesh.

"Ciaran," Madeline gently called out. "That won't help."

Ciaran withdrew his dagger. "I apologize," he said. "Please access your ordinary data and pull out the incidents in England a few weeks ago. Just the public data. I'll tell you where to go."

Lorcan obeyed. There, Ciaran guided Lorcan to pull out the news from the hotel explosion with more than twenty deaths and the incident at Fountains Abbey where more than a hundred bodies had been found.

Lorcan was speechless. He stared at his computer. "So what do you want me to do?"

"Lives are precious, regardless of whether they're human or not. You live in the Daimon Gate. I think you're open to the possibility of multiple universes and to entities living in them. Eudaiz is a universe connected to the Daimon Gate."

Lorcan nodded. "All right. I'm new here and still have to work my way through the system."

"I can give you a shortcut. Eudaiz is a universe with more than six hundred billion citizens, and it's under attack from another universe called Black Rock. The incidents in London you just saw occurred when the council members of Eudaiz tried to recruit new members and obtain weapons from Earth to protect their citizens. During the recruitment process, Madeline and I were brought to Eudaiz."

Lorcan nodded again. "I understand."

Ciaran continued, "The Daimon Gate controls passages connecting the participating universes. Black Rock is not a participating universe, but they need to transport their army to Eudaiz for an invasion. If you access the EYE, you will be able to see that they just killed thousands of citizens in District Seven. Last year, they killed more than a hundred thousand infants by blowing up our birth chambers. Because he has access to the data in the EYE, the Host knew all of this, but his hands were tied. The rule of Daimon Gate is that he must not interfere with outside affairs. But the Host wanted to help us under the radar, and that is why they kidnapped him."

"What? Who?"

"Fighters from Xiilok attacked his residence and captured him."

Lorcan darted toward the computer, attempting to look the information up.

"Don't bother, Lorcan. Your system wouldn't detect anything."

"Well, if my system can't detect them, then how can I help you?

"I don't need your system. I need your maintenance access to the EYE."

"You want to hack the EYE? That's insane."

"I am not going to steal any data. I just need to locate the entrance to Xiilok. By giving me access, you'll save the Host and a lot of people in Eudaiz, Lorcan."

Lorcan hesitated and then nodded. "All right. I can let you in, but I must be the one to handle the computer."

Ciaran nodded.

Once in, Ciaran asked Lorcan to identify locations where unidentified passengers of the gate had been spotted. They checked for the frequency of the incidents and cross-checked that data with a few other variables. Ciaran marked possible locations on the electronic map.

On Lorcan's computer screen, the data flowed, giving geographic information and the dimensions of the incidents and the landmarks of the Daimon Gate where the incidents had taken place. The computer suddenly switched to factual information. Live events flowed like movies across the screen.

Thousands and thousands of images flew past.

"What are you doing?" Ciaran asked.

"I'm not doing anything." Lorcan waved his arms in the air to show he wasn't operating the computer.

"Someone is scanning for factual information. We've been hacked. Exit the databank right now," Ciaran said.

Lorcan frantically typed on the keyboard. He shook his head, typed again. His command was deleted in front of his eyes. "What the fuck?" Lorcan exclaimed. He typed again. No text appeared on the screen. "It's not responding to my commands."

Ciaran pushed Lorcan aside and inserted his own commands. The flow of data slowed down. "It responds to mine," Ciaran said and inserted several more commands to exit the EYE databank.

The computer screen flashed. *"Top level clearance required to execute this command."*

A verification box appeared. Without hesitation, Ciaran pressed his left palm to the panel to verify.

The screen flashed. *"Signals received."*

"What? Signals of what?" Lorcan gasped.

"We're hacked. Totally screwed," Ciaran said.

CHAPTER 6

In a temporary bunker in Black Rock, located where Kyle's house used to be, the Master leaned back in his chair and smiled at the computer monitor. A female voice came across his speaker asking for communication access.

"Accepted. Text only," he said absently.

A communication panel flashed on his computer screen. The text stated, *"You're now connected."*

He grinned.

***

In the control room at Lorcan's residence in the Daimon Gate, Ciaran entered more commands. But the machine appeared to have locked him out. Hundreds of thousands of images flew across the screen, all scenes from Ciaran's life. It went going backward from the time they had entered the Daimon Gate, to London, to when he met Madeline, to his life in the past. It was like a watching movie in quick reverse.

Someone wanted information about his life.

"Ciaran! Someone or something is here. Not the Black Rock. Something new," Madeline called out. The sensation of strange creatures engulfed her.

Ciaran looked at Lorcan. "Who else is here?"

"Just my wife and me. But Orla is here all the time. Why would Madeline feel something strange just now?"

"Where is she?" Ciaran asked.

"Upstairs."

Before Ciaran and Madeline could make a move, Orla sauntered into the room. She was tall and magnificent in a red dress. Her thick long black hair cascaded over her shoulders. Then the pretty oval face stiffened, and her eyes went blank.

"Orla," Lorcan whispered. "Please don't do that to me again, baby." He approached. Orla swung her arm and hit him in the head. He fell to the ground, unconscious. Orla smirked. Then her body glowed. Light and electrical current surrounded her as if she was in a holocast.

Madeline shot at the circle of light. The laser beams bounced back as if they had struck metal.

"Guns won't work on her," Ciaran said and drew his daggers. He charged at Orla, but his dagger hit the light as if it was a brick wall. Orla spun around, throwing Ciaran against the far wall.

On the computer screen, the data was rewinding through Ciaran's childhood. It had nearly finished the retrieval process. Orla went to the computer and reached out her right arm.

"No! Don't let her get the data!" Ciaran yelled. Madeline charged at Orla. She drew her Sciphil sword and hoped it worked.

It didn't. Her sword merely made a clanking noise against the light wall.

Ciaran realized they couldn't attack the woman through the wall of light. Instead of wasting any more time with that approach, he walked around it, contemplating.

This was the technology Bran had developed during his thirty years living in the oblivion. Bran had once wanted Ciaran to use this very thing to steal data from the EYE by inserting a chip with an inexplicable amount of data storage in his palm. Someone had gained access to Bran's technology. Ciaran knew the woman had only to press her palm on the control panel, and all the data would be captured.

Orla looked at the monitor, and her eyes widened. She paused the video scroll of Ciaran's life. On the screen was a nine-year-old Ciaran, kneeling next to the bed of a girl of about thirteen or fourteen, as beautiful as an angel. The girl looked ill. The young Ciaran cried, and he was saying something. But the EYE wasn't capable of recording private conversations in private places. The location of the shot was outside a small country house.

Ciaran saw the image as well. He saw the house in the village and saw himself crying. He had been nine then, but he vividly remembered the haunting moment.

Ciaran wanted to erase the image from the screen, but Orla was in his way. He growled and stabbed again at the light circle with his daggers. There was a clank, and his daggers dropped to the floor.

Orla turned to look at Ciaran. "What did you say to that girl?" she asked.

Ciaran staggered back. Orla reached her arms out, grabbing him and throwing him to the far end of the room like a rag doll.

Ciaran stood up, holding his head. Orla stared at him blankly.

"You're not getting into my head," he grunted and slumped to the floor in pain.

Orla glanced at the computer monitor again. "What did you say to the girl?"

Madeline dashed to Ciaran's side. She held him in her arms. "Tell me what to do, Ciaran." He grabbed his head. His face turned purplish-red, the veins on his forehead swelled up, and blood trickled from his nose and ears. "Lyla, don't do this. Lyla," Ciaran said deliriously.

Madeline shook him by the shoulders. "Tell me what to do, Ciaran!"

He grunted again in pain. "Lyla, don't make me say it. Please, don't," he begged again.

"What did you say to the girl? What did she say to you? What was the spell?" Orla's eyes sparked with insanity.

Ciaran's body shook. "Madeline, I can't handle this . . . She's going to get it. She's going to pry the information out of my head. She's not Lyla," he said.

"What should I do?" Madeline asked.

"Knock me out."

Without hesitation, Madeline swung the handle of her dagger at Ciaran's temple, knocking him out cold.

Madeline turned to Orla as if she would eat the crazy woman alive if given the chance.

"You bitch!" Orla's lips curved up in a snarl, and she charged at Madeline. Madeline's sword was useless. She didn't know what to do.

The sword would not penetrate the light wall. Unbelievable! It was a Sciphil sword. She couldn't have a more powerful weapon. Then it dawned on her. This wasn't the kind of light wall they used in holocast to separate dimensions. This was a *mind* wall.

She recalled the mind maze she had dropped into the day before.

This was a similar concept. It was a mind dimension, and thus weapons of any kind in *this* dimension couldn't penetrate it. Only weapons in the mind dimension were of any use. The kind of weapon Ciaran created with his rage. He could kill with a thought. But he was unconscious at the moment and couldn't help.

She concentrated. She had to try.

In her mind, she wielded a blade.

Orla was charging at her. Madeline stood fixed in place. The blade in her mind grew larger. Sharper. And more lethal. She swung it at the light circle as Orla approached.

The light wall cracked and shattered. Orla staggered back with the impact, falling out of the light circle. She withdrew and hissed. Madeline struck her with her imagined blade again and again. Orla squealed and shrieked, excruciating sounds from hell. Madeline braced herself against the wall, yelled at the top of her lungs, and sent a final blast at Orla.

She screamed and bounced backward, falling to the floor, and her eyes rolled back in her head.

CHAPTER 7

Tadgh wished he could squirm his way into a corner or go into an eternal hibernation when he saw his girlfriend, Jo, glaring at the electronic pad stating her appointment as Sciphil Four. Even though she hadn't agreed to it, he had manipulated the system to swap Sciphil Five position to Sciphil Four.

"You agreed to this. Sciphil Five or Four is the same thing, isn't it?" Tadgh grinned.

He knew he was three years younger than Ciaran—and his maturity even less developed—but he was sure his physical appearance and intelligence were on somewhat the same level as his brother's. He had seen Ciaran pull off this smiling trick numerous times with women. It had worked on Madeline. And Jo was Madeline's best friend. They were more like sisters, growing up together in New York. So if Ciaran's trick had worked on Madeline, it had to work on Jo.

Tadgh grinned again.

But Jo didn't return his smile. Maybe he was dead wrong about his appeal to women.

Then Jo's big green eyes filled up with tears, the tears rolling down her foxy face. She shoved the electronic pad back at Tadgh and strode away quickly. Since Tadgh had taken over the Sciphil Seven position, he now lived in Sciphil Seven residence. Because Jo hadn't yet been appointed Sciphil, she stayed with him.

"Jo, can you tell me what I've done wrong? I'll fix it, I promise."

"Will I ever be good enough for you, Tadgh?"

"Wh-What? Why would you say that? What's this about?"

Jo opened her palm, revealing a glowing blue stone that Tadgh had stashed in the bottom of his dresser drawer. Tadgh's heart sank when he saw it. It was the stone holding the soul of Libby, a beautiful Eudaizian girl who had rescued Ciaran and him in Black Rock. She'd died saving them. Tadgh had admired her bravery. He thought he owed her his life, so when her soul was absorbed into the stone, he kept it.

He had told Jo about Libby. But he hadn't told her about the stone.

"Jo, I owe her my life."

"I know. I have no problem with you admiring her. Even if she had been turned into a Black Rock creature, she maintained her soul. I'm not sure I have kept mine."

"Jo, please don't say that." Tadgh suddenly grunted and bent over, holding his head. After an incident on Earth, he had developed the ability to see emotions, especially those of people he was closely connected to. He was seeing and feeling the pain in Jo memories at the moment, and the pain left him speechless.

Jo touched his face. "See. I can only bring you pain. My soul was corrupted. Kyle raped me, Tadgh. He raped my soul. And I must have given in to that. Otherwise, I would have died like his other victims."

He tried to speak, but no words passed his lips. He breathed heavily. He was dizzy. He tried to grab her. But she backed away further.

"I'll help with the Sciphil position, Tadgh. But I can't be with you. I'll only hurt you. See? How much pain can you handle? Whenever I think about Kyle, you're in pain. I'll never be able to forget him—not for the rest of my life." She moved farther away as he slumped to the ground. "I can't stand to see you in pain like this, Tadgh. I have to leave you."

She walked away.

Once she was out of his sight, Tadgh gradually regained his strength. He grabbed the communication unit to call her. He wanted to tell her that in his vision, he saw Kyle coming for her. Tadgh's emotions connected to Jo's for a very unfortunate reason—she was Kyle's victim. He had seen the emotions of Kyle's other victims as well.

The communicator stared at him blankly and wouldn't cooperate.

CHAPTER 8

Ciaran awoke to find Madeline looking at him. She brushed the hair away from his face and gently touched the bruise on his temple. "I took care of Orla. You're fine now." She smiled at him. She didn't need to say anything further—he knew what he had asked her to do hadn't been easy. He grabbed her hand and kissed it. "Thank you," he said and smiled at her.

"You're thanking me for knocking you out? What was it that Orla trying to get out of you? Who's Lyla? I saw that name in your mind first thing this morning."

"When the time comes, I'll tell you. I promise."

She was about to object, but he squeezed her hand slightly and said, "We have problems at hand that are of a higher priority. You understand that, don't you?"

She nodded reluctantly as Ciaran rushed over to the computer. He knew Madeline was watching him from behind, and he hadn't given her a satisfactory answer, but it would have to do for now. The computer appeared to be secured. He hunched over it to retrieve additional data and then entered numerous codes and commands to lock it securely.

They entered the next room where, to Ciaran's amusement, Madeline had managed to tie Orla and Lorcan securely to chairs. Their mouths were gagged with rags.

"I understand you're upset because we tied you up in your own house. But we have a serious situation here, and if I don't get an agreement from you, I can't let you go," Ciaran said. "Care to hear me out?" Lorcan nodded. Orla grumbled and snarled. She glared at Ciaran.

"Your wife doesn't seem to want to cooperate, Lorcan. Okay, let's do it this way. I'll tell you what I've got, and you decide whether or not you want to cooperate." Ciaran didn't wait for a response but continued, "While I was searching the databank, I noted you had requested that Orla come to live in the gate with you as an ordinary human. You reported her as a housewife without an official job. Which is fine for the EYE. The system only observes and records—it doesn't analyze. It can't draw the conclusion that Orla is a sorceress belonging to the nastiest branch in Ireland that claims to use black magic."

Orla's eyes teared up. Lorcan shook his head and signaled he wanted to talk. Ciaran pulled the rags out of his mouth.

"She's not a sorceress—has never been and never will be. She didn't mean to hurt you. She's never done that before. You have to trust me. Something possessed her and made her do that."

Ciaran smiled. "I know it wasn't her who wanted the data. But that's not relevant to what I'm saying here. The Daimon Gate recruits the most righteous men to be their gatekeepers. That's why cheating the system has such a severe penalty. I take my hat off to you for your bravery, Lorcan. But a cheat is a cheat, and a cheat doesn't deserve trust."

Tears rolled down Orla's face. Ciaran approached her. "I know you won't scream now, so this will be more comfortable for you." He removed the cloth from her mouth.

"I'm sorry, Lorcan. I was possessed. I couldn't control it," she sobbed.

"No, baby, don't cry. The situation called for it. It wasn't your fault. If we're doomed now, so be it. We'll die together. Better to be in here than out there. I love you, Orla."

Ciaran saw Madeline had tears in her eyes, and he winked at her. "How about I offer you this? I'll leave with Madeline now to go to Xiilok. I will never reveal the fact that Orla is—or was—a sorceress. On your end, you have to forget what you saw, keep our conversation a secret, and erase all traces of some alterations I made in the databank."

"You did what?" Lorcan yelled.

"I don't have the time to erase the signs of what I did. So why don't you do that for me?" Ciaran deadpanned.

"You erased the data? The part of your childhood—"

"Ah, ah." Ciaran wagged a finger in front of Lorcan's face. "That's the information you're supposed to *forget*. You forget that, and I'll forget Orla practiced black magic. Do we have a deal?"

"Fuck your deal, Ciaran."

"All right then." Ciaran stood up to leave.

"Okay, okay," Lorcan muttered.

Ciaran nodded and untied Lorcan. Madeline untied Orla.

"You don't know what it was that possessed you? What wanted to get my data?" Ciaran asked Orla.

Orla shook her head. "One thing I can tell you, though, he's a sorcerer, and he used the same technique my family used—black magic. Whether or not you're a believer, I'm telling, it's nasty stuff."

Ciaran nodded. "Thank you. I appreciate the information."

CHAPTER 9

Ciaran and Madeline passed a dimensional doorway where, according to the map, there had been many incidents of illegal travelers entering the Daimon Gate. The ground was black and slightly spongy and sticky on the feet.

"I guess it's logical that they wouldn't post a sign saying 'Welcome to Xiilok' here," Madeline joked. She stomped her foot on the ground. "What *is* this? Mud?"

Ciaran rubbed the bottom of his shoe on the ground. "It's not mud, and it's not organic material." He crouched to have a closer look at the ground. "It only covers this area right here." He pointed to an old tree standing next to a well. "Over there, the ground is different. I'm guessing this is a welcome mat of sorts. Don't let your skin contact anything here."

They approached the tree and the well. On the tree trunk, they saw some letters carved into the bark, looking something like 'ττίνω'. Madeline frowned. "Are those alien symbols?"

Ciaran shook his head. "It's Greek for *drink* if I'm not mistaken."

"You speak Greek?"

"No. Not really. But I studied the language for reading purposes."

"They want to welcome us with a drink from this?" Madeline pointed to the well. "Hell no."

"Careful." Ciaran pulled Madeline back and stepped in front of her.

From nowhere, two creatures appeared. It seemed they had stepped out from another dimension—or simply from thin air. They were small, standing as high as Madeline's waist, and had human shape. Their skin glowed a shimmery yellow. They had huge eyes, round faces, and a line across the face that Madeline figured was a mouth of some kind. They didn't look or act hostile, but they stood and sized up Madeline and Ciaran with measured glances.

A stream of melodic words came out of their mouths. Madeline was positive they weren't singing. "That's not Greek, is it, Ciaran?"

"No. That's definitely an alien language." Ciaran smiled and palmed his daggers.

One of the creatures pointed at the well. Another stream of words flowed forth.

"Sorry, we don't speak your language," Ciaran said.

The creatures looked at each other. One of them mangled the word, "Earth." It looked at Ciaran and Madeline.

Madeline nodded. "Earth," she said and smiled graciously.

The creatures waved their hands absently as if they had lost their interest in the two of them and then walked away, disappearing into the thin air from whence they'd come.

"What the heck?" Madeline exclaimed.

"At least they weren't hostile," Ciaran said and pulled out his map. He knew very well the map wouldn't work here, but he tried his luck anyway. He shook his head, looking at the blank screen. "Do you have any sense of where we should be going from here?"

Madeline closed her eyes and concentrated. She tried to sense Conan. She had only met him once, and that was when she was under duress. She sensed nothing. She tried again. Around her, the environment buzzed with confusing noises, senses, and distorted shapes. The buzzes became louder and clearer. Then she felt Ciaran pull her arms. She opened her eyes and saw a group of five men approaching them. They had familiar human shapes and sizes and looked human except for their eyes. There were multicolored worms swimming in their irises.

A tall man wearing cowboy boots and a scarred leather jacket approached and stared at Madeline's and Ciaran's faces. Madeline knew he was focusing on their eyes to see if they had the familiar worm-whirling irises. The man cleared his throat and spoke in American English with a thick Southern accent. "You're not Xiiloks. You got a job for us?"

Ciaran nodded. "Indeed, we do."

The man raised an eyebrow. "British? I could work for some British pounds. I have fond memories of the last time I traveled there. What's the job?"

"There's a gatekeeper in the Daimon Gate I want you to capture and deliver to us."

The man sneered. "You can't afford that kind of job."

"How much do you want?"

An Asian man standing at the back retorted, "Don't waste your time, Nick. We can't take Daimon Gate jobs. Let's go."

"Hey, don't call my name out in front of outsiders. I'll kick your ass out of the group!" the tall man exclaimed. "I didn't say I wanted the job. I just want to cheat a few pounds off them, you idiot!"

"Why can't you take a Daimon Gate job?" Ciaran asked.

Nick turned to look at Ciaran and Madeline. "Why would I tell you that?"

"I can pay you for the information."

Nick grinned. "Much better. What do you want to know?"

"Who in Xiilok can take a Daimon Gate job?"

A large man spoke up, "He can't give you that information, either." The large man pushed his way toward the front. He looked Ciaran and Madeline up and down and continued, "Not that we *can't* take the job. It's just not worth the risk. We're outlaws, but we have standards. Xiilok is our second chance, and there isn't a third one." Before he turned away, he tilted his head and nodded to his left. "Let's go, boys."

Ciaran noticed the Asian man muttering something to a quiet man behind him. The man looked to be in his forties and wore a black robe with a hood. He didn't look like the other members of the group. *Maybe he's not human,* Ciaran mused. The man cast a glance at Ciaran and Madeline and then turned away. The group of men left, turning into a dimension, and soon Ciaran and Madeline could no longer see them.

Ciaran grabbed Madeline's hand and walked to the left. There was a canvas of thick jungle and mountains at the horizon. When they approached a tree, Ciaran reached his hand out to touch the trunk. His hand went right through the tree.

"So this is all an illusion. I guess only Xiilok citizens can see the real thing."

Madeline walked toward a rock.

"Wait." Ciaran grabbed her. "Don't walk away from me. This area is full of dimensional gates, doors, and traps."

Madeline pushed at the rock. "This one is real," she said as the rock remained solid at her push.

They heard a whooshing sound, and a ball rolled out from another dimension and stopped at Ciaran's feet. As he realized it wasn't a ball but a head, it melted into a black puddle, and writhing worms piled up on his shoes.

Ciaran yelped and leaped away, shaking his feet to get the worms off. He wiped his shoes on what looked like grass until he was absolutely sure there were none remaining. Madeline stood gawking at him.

"I detest slithering things," he said shakily.

Madeline approached him. She grabbed his hands and found them clammy. She pulled him to her and held him, finding his heart racing. She knew he was ophidiophobic, but she thought his fear of snakes came from a fear of their bites and venom, not from their slithering movements. Madeline wanted to chuckle but withheld the urge so as not to be inconsiderate. She found Ciaran's phobia oddly adorable.

Ciaran eased away from her embrace. "Well, this is embarrassing," he said.

"No, warrior. I'm glad there's something you're afraid of. Just like humans!"

A shower of body parts poured out from a dimensional hole and flopped onto the ground near them. Madeline pushed at Ciaran, and they backed away. From the other dimension, half a dozen of rotten creatures that looked like zombies appeared. They checked the body parts and looked satisfied— at least as much they could tell from their zombie expressions. One of them glanced up and saw Madeline and Ciaran.

"Run!" Ciaran tugged at Madeline. He didn't think they had any advantage fighting the zombies on Earth, let alone in another universe.

"They have Conan, Ciaran," Madeline whispered. "I can feel it. They have him."

Ciaran's jaw clenched. He pushed Madeline behind him and waited for the zombies to come closer.

"French or English, your choice, but I don't speak any other languages," Ciaran said to the group.

The zombie standing at the front smirked. "You're lucky I'm fond of English. I guess being trapped under this skin for such a long time," he gestured at himself, "you can't tell my race anymore. But it hardly matters now. In Xiilok, this is as good as it's going to get." He raised his bony hand and signaled.

A small zombie standing at the back moved up. "Carlo?" the small zombie said. Carlo cast a dismissive glance on him.

"Since when do you move so fast? Just wait there." Carlo looked at Ciaran. "I can give you proof of the work done, but you have to give me proof that you've got the merchandise in exchange."

Oh hell, Madeline thought. She knew they had Conan, and they thought she and Ciaran were the ones who had hired them. She had no idea how Ciaran was going to handle this. She hoped the worm-related incident hadn't shaken his quick thinking too much.

"What proof of the man do you have for me?" Ciaran asked.

"How about something that belongs to him?" Carlo said.

"Bring me his wrist unit," Ciaran said.

Carlo arched something that looked like it used to be an eyebrow. "And what do I get in return?"

"Nothing now. My information indicates you've got the wrong man. You won't have the merchandise before you give me the right man."

"The wrong man? That's impossible. I got him myself, from his residence," Carlo snarled.

"Well, you can keep him," Ciaran replied. "I won't pay for the wrong job." He turned around, wrapping his arm around Madeline's shoulders to walk away.

"I'll kill him," Carlo growled.

Ciaran waved his hand absently and kept walking.

"All right, I'll bring you his wrist unit."

Ciaran turned around. "You're playing games with me, and I don't care for that. The wrist unit isn't enough."

"What?" Carlo yelled as other zombies pulled out their knives, daggers, swords and spears, brandishing the weapons in front of them.

"Killing us will get you nothing. Did you take the man who was in the long reception room, the one sitting at a long table having tea? On his right was a control unit, and at the far end of that room was a corridor that led to their control center. If your answer is yes to anything I've just said, you definitely have the wrong man. Don't bother with his wrist unit."

Carlo was incredulous. The description he'd just been given was precisely what the room had been like.

CHAPTER 10

Madeline chuckled to herself—the idiotic zombie didn't know Conan was Ciaran's father. Conan had decorated the reception hall of his residence in the Daimon Gate so that it looked exactly like Mon Ciel, their home at Henley-on-Thames. Ciaran had told her his father had reproduced every small detail of Mon Ciel's Great Reception room and that it hurt him to think of how much his father had missed home all these years.

"The man matches the description you gave me."

"I can show you ten men that match that description. The Host of the Daimon Gate has cloned many decoys," Ciaran said.

"Why didn't you inform us?"

"I wasn't aware he used decoys in his own home. But I've heard that people received communication from him just this morning, and he attended his meetings at central. Now it could very well be a decoy that they're using at the Daimon Gate because they don't want to announce that their Host is missing, but I still need to verify the man in the flesh."

"You're fucking around with us," Carlo snarled.

Ciaran shrugged. "I'm not the boss. I just report what I see and can verify. Now I'll have to tell my boss that you've shown me nothing." Ciaran turned around again.

"All right. Follow us—and don't fool around in here." The zombies walked through a dimensional gate. Ciaran grabbed Madeline's hand tightly as if afraid she'd make a wrong turn and disappear right in front of him.

They stepped into another dimension.

The ground in this dimension was more solid, and the scenery around them seemed more real. They were walking along the edge of a cliff, snaking down to a valley. In the distance, Ciaran and Madeline saw small residences. At the base of the cliff, they approached a prominent temple-like one. The zombies led them straight to the entrance.

In the hall, Carlo gestured toward a side door. Ciaran glanced back toward the entrance, making mental notes of the exits. The side door slid open, and two small zombies led Conan out. His hands were tied behind him, and his eyes locked with Ciaran's. Neither spoke a word, but Madeline knew there was information being exchanged between father and son.

Ciaran approached Conan. "I'm sent to verify that you are the true Host of the Daimon Gate. I'd like to see your wrist unit." Conan turned around, showing the rope which bound his wrists. Ciaran spoke to Carlo, "Would you mind untying him?"

Carlo was busy talking to another zombie who had just entered from the side door. He waved his hand absently. The zombie standing next to Conan cut the rope off.

Ciaran smiled. He had opened his mouth and was just about to speak when Carlo cut in. "I see we've got the wrong man after all." Then he grinned evilly at Ciaran.

Ciaran immediately grabbed Conan and Madeline, pushing them behind him protectively.

The other zombies surrounded them, aiming their weapons at the group. "Well now, Ciaran LeBlanc, king of Eudaiz, thank you for making my job so easy," Carlo remarked while he paced back and forth behind his minions.

They closed in. Madeline pulled her Sciphil sword—it glowed in her hands. She swung it, and it sent forth a wedge of energy, pushing the zombies backward.

"Give me your sword, Madeline," Ciaran said.

She handed it over, but the sword stopped glowing when his hands touched it. When he swung Madeline's Sciphil sword, it had no impact whatsoever on the zombies. It was merely an ordinary piece of sharp metal in Ciaran's hands.

The zombies laughed hysterically.

Ciaran gave Madeline her sword and pulled out his daggers. "I hope your last laugh is satisfying," Ciaran said, charging at the zombies blocking the doorway. With a few swings of his daggers, their body parts scattered on the floor and turned into murky puddles swimming with worms.

The three made their way to the door, Conan brandishing one of Madeline's daggers and

Madeline guarding their backs with her Sciphil sword. They made it out of the temple without much difficulty as the zombies didn't have combat skills.

In front of the temple, a sea of zombies swarmed at them from the right. They'd arrived from the left, so it made sense to run back that way. They raced as fast as they could. Ciaran saw a wedge of light in the distance.

"Madeline, does this feel like the way to the Daimon Gate?"

"Yes," she confirmed.

They headed toward the light, but the ground cracked and split just behind Ciaran, separating him from Madeline and Conan. The ground on which Madeline and Conan stood shifted backward, floating like a flying disc.

"Ciaran!" Madeline cried out.

Ciaran looked back to see his wife and father being carried away in the opposite direction. He looked down toward his feet—maybe he was the one being carried away. Madeline swung her sword, desperately protecting his father from the approaching zombies. Her eyes, those big brown eyes that he always found himself drowning in, were begging him to get them back together again.

Ciara looked down. The crack between them had turned into a muddy black river, swimming with slithering worms and maggots. He looked up again and saw Madeline and his father being whisked farther away on the piece of floating ground. Desperate to reach them, Ciaran jumped from his safe piece of earth and dashed across the maggot river, holding his breath and trying to control his fear.

He ran.

And ran.

But the more he ran, the farther away Madeline and his father seemed to get. He thought that odd, so he paused. He stopped running right in the middle of the maggots. When he stopped, the piece of land that carried Madeline and Conan stopped as well. Madeline jumped off and ran toward Ciaran. Conan followed. Ciaran stood very still. He knew if he moved, there would be an impact on Madeline and Conan. He stood there while the worms crawled up his shoes.

"Well, aren't you a strong one?" Carlo whispered into Ciaran's ear. Ciaran whirled around to see the zombie standing right behind him with a crooked grin on his face. Behind him was a sea of the undead. "Come with me, Ciaran, and I'll let Madeline and the Host live," Carlo croaked.

Without a word, Ciaran swung his daggers. Carlo blocked them. Another zombie flew at Ciaran, its sword aimed at his side. Ciaran sidestepped it, pushed Carlo aside, and swung his daggers once more. As the rotting corpse's sword whizzed toward his side, Ciaran cut off its head. Maggots spilled from the severed neck.

"If you'd like to keep that head on your shoulders a bit longer, you'd better run and hide behind your pathetic soldiers," Ciaran suggested to Carlo. Carlo growled then waved, signaling his zombies to stop their attack. Carlo himself then advanced on Ciaran. Ciaran could feel the warm blood gushing from his wounded side. Carlo smirked and continued his advance. Ciaran aimed one of his daggers at Carlo's abdomen. Blocking the swing, Carlo looked down in an attempt to locate and block the second dagger, but Ciaran outsmarted him and plunged it into his head.

Carlo roared as his body quickly melted, raining writhing maggots onto Ciaran like water from a fountain. He swatted them away and dove to the ground where he'd been standing, but the earth started caving in. He tried to jump aside, but he was too late. He was sucked down into the sinking ground. He heard Madeline screaming his name, but there was nothing he could do.

Everything turned into blackness.

CHAPTER 11

Ciaran dropped to the ground of a familiar place. He scrambled up to his feet and stood still to regain his bearings. He recognized this place. His stolen capsule from Black Rock was shot down here before Sizx had picked him up.

He'd been shot out from a dimensional hole and had somehow ended up here. There was something about District Six that warranted a closer look. But for now, he needed to make a move. Madeline and his father were still back at Xiilok.

He heard the faint sound of an incoming capsule. He wondered if it was Sizx, coming to give him assistance, but he quickly brushed that thought away.

The capsule landed close to where he stood. Emerging from the capsule was, indeed, Sizx. To Ciaran's relief, following her was Ayana.

"Where have you been, Ciaran?" Ayana asked.

"How did you know I was here?" Ciaran asked.

Ayana glanced at Sizx.

"Oh, not again. Sizx! Where?" Ciaran asked.

Sizx approached and pulled at a small button on the side pocket of Ciaran's jacket. She placed the button on her upturned palm.

"Where else did you tag me, Sizx? I don't like this at all," Ciaran growled.

"That's all I've got on you," Sizx said and looked at the ground. He didn't believe her. Not one bit. But there was no time to deal with such trivial matters now.

"Why are you looking for me, Ayana?"

"We have to replace Sciphil Four since Kyle might be dead. It's been scheduled for tomorrow."

"Why the rush?"

"It's not our decision. Officiation works on an astronomical timetable when all the right elements line up at a precise moment."

"Who should we appoint?"

"Josephine Cassidy."

"Tadgh's girlfriend. I've lined her up for Sciphil Five position."

"Yes. I've spoken to Tadgh, and he promised to convince Jo to swap. But we need you to conduct the officiation."

Ciaran nodded. "I understand. I have some personal business to handle. But I'll make sure I'm at the officiation. Now I need to borrow your capsule and all communication equipment available to contact my network on Earth."

Sizx grinned. "I'm on it."

"You're not playing any tricks on me? Planting more bugs on me, Sizx?"

"No, Ciaran."

***

Madeline ran backward, holding her sword tight and protecting Conan from the back. Zombies were everywhere. They cringed with every swing of her sword, but they wouldn't stop following. She looked at the sea of them, unsure of how to get out of this messy situation.

She had seen the piece of land break off and carry Ciaran away. She'd watched as he was sucked into the wormhole, her nerves along with him. As much as she loved her children, she wasn't sure if she could carry on without him. Her sixth sense was no longer working—she couldn't tell if Ciaran was alive. Nothing seemed to work properly in Xiilok.

A zombie backed Madeline and Conan into a space where two large rocks were wedged together, effectively cornering them. This could be the end of them.

"I'm so sorry, Conan. I just don't see how we can get out of this."

"I should be the one saying sorry, Madeline. Your children will be orphans."

Madeline felt a lump in her throat. She thought of Ciaran—of her children and the family she hadn't yet had a chance to cherish.

The zombies leaned away with each swing of her sword, but then they advanced again. In only a short time, Madeline would use up all of her strength. Once she gave up, the decaying creatures would be all over them. She and Conan would die in blood and gore in the middle of no man's land.

Suddenly, the sea of zombies wavered and seemed disturbed. They turned, panting and disoriented. Madeline perked up. She sensed her mate. It was him. It was Ciaran! He was here. He had come back for her.

"Ciaran is back," she said.

Conan tried to peer over the army of zombies, but he saw no sign of his son. What he did see was an army of creatures attacking the zombies from behind them. They slashed, stabbed, and trampled the undead. Zombies left and right disintegrated into heaps of worms and maggots. The ones closest to Madeline and Conan hurried away as fast as they could.

The disintegration of the sea of zombies revealed hundreds of yellow creatures of all different shapes and sizes. Madeline recognized them as those she and Ciaran had encountered upon their arrival at Xiilok. She saw the five men who had refused to take a Daimon Gate job. But no Ciaran.

The army of creatures suddenly split, and from the back, Ciaran moved toward her. Her magnificent warrior. The king of Eudaiz. Madeline was ecstatic. She refrained from running to him and leaping into his arms, thinking it better to walk gracefully. But then she threw caution to the wind, galloping to him and allowing him to sweep her off her feet.

Madeline chuckled. "I guess you bought the entire Xiilok army."

"Almost. All but the zombies. They're all dead—for the second time," he joked and smiled at her. They kissed while the army of yellow creatures roared in excitement.

***

Back at the Daimon Gate, Ciaran left Madeline in the residence while he went to talk to his parents. He wanted to check on his children in the birth chamber before going back to Eudaiz with Madeline. He felt uneasy when he learned that Moira had left suddenly to go back to iilos before they got back from Xiilok. Moira always had an agenda.

The birth chamber was quiet.

His children were healthy. He wondered how they would look like when they finally came out of those boxes. Then he noticed a small, round box attached to the frame of the window looking into the birth chamber. There was a small note on top.

"To Ciaran. Moira."

He took the box and carefully positioned it far from his face before opening it. There was nothing inside the box except another note written on a piece of paper. He picked up the note. It said, "You cheated, Ciaran. What I gave you, I can always take back. You have five days to come to iilos and talk to me."

There was a stabbing pain in his brain as small pool of red liquid leaked out from the bottom of the box and absorbed into his right palm.

He dropped the box.

He could see the liquid pooling into a large drop underneath his skin. It was quickly absorbed into his blood and pumped immediately via his veins through his entire body.

He blacked out.

He came about quickly. Or at least he thought it was quick because he was still alone in the birth chamber. The he heard footsteps and Madeline's voice heading toward the chamber. Ciaran scrambled to his feet.

He glanced around him. Everything was intact. He hadn't fallen on anything on the way down. He looked at his palm. No trace of the poison. He thought there had most likely been no effect on his appearance—for now.

"Ciaran," Madeline called for him at the door.

"Yes." He turned around and looked at her, shoving the piece of paper into his pocket at the same time.

"What's happening in here?"

"Nothing." He looked at Madeline. "I was just checking on the children."

CHAPTER 12

They walked into the grand hall of Sciphil Three's residence. She could call this home. As Sciphil One, Madeline had her own residence. But as a wife, her home was here, with Ciaran.

The hallway was colder than usual. The robot didn't scurry out to greet them. Or maybe it did, and she just wasn't paying attention. Something wasn't sitting well in her mind.

Ciaran hadn't spoken all the way back here from the Daimon Gate. Her psychic ability wasn't working at the moment, regardless of how much she tried to trigger it. She wanted to peek into Ciaran's mind to see what he was thinking about.

All she could tell now was that he was hiding something from her.

They entered the bed chamber. It was still early in the evening. Maybe when she sensed a friendly aura, she would start a conversation and ask him about what had happened.

Then she saw it. A flash of Ciaran's thoughts. Just one word—poison.

Calm down! she told herself. It mightn't mean anything. She walked around the room and stared out the window at the plastic-like trees in the garden. *Has he been poisoned? By whom? And why didn't he tell her?* Her mind raced through thousands of questions and ended up with nothing but confusion for an answer.

Ciaran always had a reason for what he did. And when there was a reason, there would be reasoning. She would do just that. She turned around and saw he had removed his armor and changed into casual clothes. She cleared her throat and asked, "Are you okay?"

Ciaran's eyes darkened instantly. She could feel her body tense up. She should have known. He was way too smart for her to play mind games with him. *Damn!* she cursed silently and waited for his verbal blows.

"You spied into my mind, and I don't care for that. I'd like some privacy, Madeline."

She raised her arms in the air. "Privacy? More like secrets. And secrets don't do our marriage any good!"

"Are you threatening me with our marriage?" His voice was dangerously low.

She put her hands on her hips. "You're the one threatening our marriage. You woke up in the morning with the name Lyla in your head. Turns out she isn't a secret mistress. But she might be your childhood sweetheart. Which is fine by me, by the way. And then you left me defending your father against gazillions of zombies—"

"I didn't leave you. You knew the situation!"

"It was hard to see. I was prepared to die because it just wasn't possible to win that fight."

"I came back and got you out of it, didn't I?"

"Now that was the problem, Ciaran. In such a short period of time, you were able to get your contact from Earth to cough up the money and buy that army. I know the LeBlancs have resources. But to deal *that* fast, you've got to have someone waiting on the sidelines at your beck and call—a woman. A secret woman that you refer to as your 'privacy.'"

"This is crazy, Madeline. Where does that ridiculous assumption come from?" Ciaran raised his voice.

He'd never raised his voice with her before. She pressed on. "It's not an assumption. I saw the word *poison* in your mind just now. Didn't you just think about that?"

Silence.

"Whoever your mistress is probably got pissed because you're not with her but with me. So pissed that she poisoned you in revenge. Only a woman would do such thing. Can you tell me that there isn't poison in your body right now? Do I have to get the robot to scan you?"

Silence.

She sighed, pulled out her lowest card, and manufactured a tear. "I rest my case," she said. "I should have known the LeBlancs were out of my league."

Ciaran approached. "It's not what you think."

"I don't know what to think anymore."

He pulled her into his arms. "It was Moira. Somehow she figured out I bluffed to make her help you deliver the babies. She poisoned me. She gave me five days to negotiate."

"What does she want?"

"I designed a computer program called the Mind Ripper to operate super soldiers. She wants the program. So I lied. I told her I've got the program. But I haven't gotten a chance to complete it before we left London"

She sighed. "I know how she figured it out."

"How?"

"At the Daimon Gate, before we left for Xiilok, you said we weren't at a stage where we could develop super soldiers. She must have heard that and put two and two together. Now, you don't have the program. What should we do?"

"Not yet, but I will have it. It's only a matter of time, Madeline."

"Can you do it in five days?"

"Madeline, that's not the point. Super soldiers can't be handled by just anyone. If used for the wrong purposes, the consequences would be tremendous. Whatever the reason she has for wanting to use super soldiers, I'm sure it is completely selfish and wrong. So I'm not going to crawl back to iilos and let her blackmail me for a pathetic antidote."

"What if you can't figure out the antidote? Are you willing to die to protect the integrity of the cosmos' military, or your code of conduct, or whatever it is you're protecting? And you aren't even the king yet. There are truckloads of badasses out there who want you dead. This is too damn convenient for them."

"I'll figure out the antidote. I will not negotiate with her and let her terrorize me, Eudaiz, or any other universes."

She nodded. "So I will have to live in fear until you sort this out. Five days, right? I can handle this." More tears rolled down her face. She wasn't sure if they were real tears this time. They might be. She reached up and wrapped her arms around his shoulders. "Promise you'll do your best. Never leave me and the children."

He bent down and nuzzled into the crook of her neck. "I promise."

From behind him, she took a square patch of sedative out of her hand and slapped it on the back of his neck.

"Madeline!"

Before Ciaran could reach up to peel off the patch, she tightened her arms around him and wrestled him toward the bed. She knew he could easily throw her into the far wall to free himself. But he would never hurt her, so he just wriggled slightly. She only needed two seconds.

"Let go, Madeline. Don't do this."

When his legs hit the bed, he was thrown off balance and fell onto it on his back. She jumped on top of him and pinned his arms down. She looked into his beautiful eyes which had gone instantly opaque. *Eudaiz's drugs are effective*, she thought and silently thanked Liam, their new Eudaizian doctor. Ciaran's struggles stopped. His face went lax. His body shut down.

Madeline wiped a strand of hair from Ciaran's face. Her husband looked so tired. She kissed him and climbed off the bed. She swiveled his legs onto the bed and pulled the blanket up to cover him.

She engaged the control panel and then realized she didn't know how to operate the machine to do what she needed to do.

She had no choice but to call Sizx for assistance.

CHAPTER 13

Later, in a capsule, Sizx manned the control panel and glanced at Madeline's bare wrist. "I guess you wanted this trip to be off the radar."

Madeline smiled. "I appreciate your help. If I knew how to drive this stupid capsule, I wouldn't have bothered you."

"No bother at all. You're a Sciphil. It's my duty to help you."

"Thank you."

They arrived at Sciphil Six in no time. This residence hosted a dimensional gateway to iilos, where Moira lived. She asked Sizx to wait and went inside. Madeline was no stranger to this. She walked into the dimensional gate and then stepped out into the hall of an Irish country house.

Although she had been in excruciating pain on her first visit, Madeline remembered every single step she had taken. Moira was waiting at the end of the hall, her face radiant, and her flaming red hair stunning.

"You're brave to come and see me alone. What will stop me from snapping your neck right here?" Moira asked.

"I'm more useful to you alive. It's cliché, but true."

Moira smiled.

"You poisoned my husband. That's low. But I'm here to give you the bad news because you don't know Ciaran, and I also have a deal to make with you. So do you want the bad news or the deal first?"

"Let's sort out the bad news to ensure we aren't going ahead with a deal in a sour mood."

Madeline nodded. "The bad news for you is that Ciaran will never negotiate with you, whether he finds the antidote or not. Your poison doesn't give you any bargaining power over him."

Moira arched an eyebrow. "And you're going to let him die?"

"His life. His choice. You threatened his innocent children. You threatened his wife, and now his own life. All for a program to operate super soldiers. A man like Ciaran would never stoop so low. You're not of his caliber. You're dirt to him."

Moira slapped her across the face so hard that she fell to the floor. Madeline stood up, wiped the blood from her split lip. "That was unnecessary. But given you're Ciaran's ancestor, I'm not going to return the blow."

"And what is your stupid deal?" Moira growled.

"I can see you're taking the news well. All right, what I just said to you was from Ciaran's perspective—a man's perspective. I came here as a woman, a wife, and a mother. Ignoring the fact that you slapped me, we could be friends if you had even one of those three attributes."

"Bullshit!"

Madeline smiled. "Well, that makes you a woman. And you were Pierre LeBlanc's wife—the wife of the first king of Eudaiz. Isn't that something? Two out of three. Now on to the third . . ." Madeline could see Moira's face burning. It was almost as red as her hair. She looked as if she was about to lunge at Madeline again. Madeline raised a hand. "If you hit me again, I *will* return the attack. Cat fights are never pretty. So save both of us the ordeal and hear me out."

Moira stepped back and slowly regained her poise and composure.

Madeline continued, "What would make a woman like you hang around for five hundred years after your husband died, living in this lonely castle and hustling across the cosmos to build an army of super soldiers? I can only think of one reason— guilt."

"Don't you dare psychoanalyze me. Get to the point. What is your deal?" Moira asked angrily.

"Thank you for confirming my suspicions. So this has something to do with your offspring, with love, and maybe with your husband—"

"I'm warning you, I am not a patient woman. What do you offer in return for the antidote? That's what you want, isn't it?"

"I can't make a deal without knowing your bottom line. What do you want the soldiers for? Ciaran might not understand you, but I do."

"How do I know you'd understand? Who are you to think you'd understand what I went through?"

"I was a field journalist in New York for ten years before I met Ciaran. I wrote about women and their problems in relationships and family. Not the how-to-date-a man-in-ten-days or how-to-scam-a-millionaire-for-inheritance kind of problems, but the kind that break a person, break a life . . . break a heart. The kind of problem that you are dealing with."

Madeline could see her ten years of experience in journalism paying off—she was about to shake loose the five hundred years' worth of steel fence surrounding this woman.

"What happened, Moira? Why do you need super soldiers?"

Moira's eyes stared into the distance for a moment as if her mind had drifted back to a painful past. "Five hundred years ago, ten of us survived the Daimon Gate. We were the first humans to arrive in Eudaiz. Pierre built the first Sciphil council of nine. He wouldn't let me be one of them. The LeBlanc men are very protective of their women—you know that."

Madeline smiled as she thought of her husband. He was definitely protective of her, but he would never hold her back from accomplishing what she wanted just because she was a woman. Madeline knew the situation in England five hundred years ago would have been very different.

"Pierre negotiated with the Daimon Gate Host to put the Sciphil tests in place to screen future Sciphils and protect Eudaiz. At that point, he discovered the power of the Red Stage of the Daimon Gate. Children conceived during the Red Stage were considered to be the best beings in the cosmos."

"He wanted an heir?"

Moira shook her head. "I wanted him to have the best child as an heir, so I suggested we go back to the Daimon Gate."

Madeline shuddered, remembering the confusion, sexual temptation, and brutal attacks from all kind of creatures at the Red Stage. If it hadn't been for their unbreakable love for each other, that test would have broken Ciaran and killed her. But they succeeded. They survived. Obviously, Moira and Pierre hadn't been that lucky.

A tear rolled down Moira's face. "There was another man." Then more tears came. "I need to believe I was faithful to my husband. He didn't believe me. He died thinking I had betrayed him . . ." She broke down and cried so hard that Madeline and to wait for a moment until she settled.

"You should know whether or not you were faithful to your husband. Why do you need to *believe?*"

"It was a world of hallucination. And I was the one who had to make the choice," Moira said.

Madeline vividly remembered the room full of nasty creatures waiting to claw Ciaran into pieces. He had been the one who had to make the choice. Hundreds of creatures had wanted to kill Ciaran, and they were all looked exactly like her. Ciaran had had two choices. He could either kill the creatures or consummate with one of them. If he didn't choose, they'd eat him alive. If he made the wrong choice, he'd be killed. So he'd killed many of them. But somehow, in the jungle of creatures that all looked like her, he had recognized the real her.

That was how they had survived.

"Did you . . . choose the wrong one?" Madeline asked with caution.

"No. I knew who I consummated with. And it was Pierre." Moira covered her face and stayed still for a short moment, then she looked at Madeline. "I did have a moment of weakness, though. I thought of the other man. Just one thought. But it clouded my judgment and contaminated our consummation. In my heart, I knew I had never betrayed my husband. I knew whose child I bore. But the man made Pierre believed I had been unfaithful . . ."

Moira buried her face in her hands again. When she looked back at Madeline, she swore the woman had aged ten years right in front of her. Moira continued, "Pierre was injured in the fight during the test. He didn't treat himself well, and he died because of it. We had a daughter. She was still in the box when a man snatched her and disappeared."

Moira laughed bitterly. "Before he died, Pierre said he forgave me and made me promise to take care of our daughter." She shook her head. "I didn't need his forgiveness. I hadn't betrayed him. I have never betrayed my husband. After he died, I searched for our daughter. I don't know how long it was before I finally got the news that she might be in Xiilok."

She raised her arm and showed Madeline a wristband. "This dimensional resistance has kept me alive and unchanged across all dimensions. And it prevented me from entering Xiilok."

"Who was the man? Is he living in Xiilok, too?"

Moira shook her head. "He was one of the ten people who first came to Eudaiz. I killed him with

Pierre's king Sciphil sword. So now I need super soldiers to travel with into Xiilok because ordinary ones cannot survive that place. I need to find my daughter."

"After five hundred years? You have the dimensional resistance. But your daughter wouldn't have it."

Moira looked at Madeline. "In my heart, I know she'd alive... Ciaran isn't going to give me the army for this, is he?"

"I don't think so." Madeline understood Moira's predicament but knew Ciaran was right. Hers was a personal reason. It was not a legitimate reason to raise an army of super soldiers. Madeline thought she might have done the same thing if she were Moira. But Ciaran wasn't the kind of man who would make a decision on a whim. He was a man with great responsibilities, and he would always consider the interest of the greater cause.

"How about I promise you I'll go into Xiilok and search for your daughter? I've got some skills, and I've been there. I survived that universe and rescued Conan from an army of zombies."

Moira absently wiped the tears from her face. She opened a compartment, pulled out a hidden control panel, and entered some commands. The machine issued a small square patch. "This is the antidote for Ciaran." She gave it to Madeline.

"You believe me? Just like that?"

Moira shook her head. "No. If I don't expect anything, I won't be disappointed. I know you think my daughter must be dead after all these years. But a mother's instinct tells me otherwise. I appreciate you listening to me and perhaps believing me. So I give you the antidote as a token of my gratitude. I will continue searching for my daughter."

"I'll help look for your daughter after Ciaran gets through his coronation."

Moira nodded and smiled. "I wish him all the best."

Madeline turned to leave, but then she thought of something else and turned back. "You know what, Moira? I don't think you'd need super soldiers to rescue your daughter if she's in Xiilok."

Moira arched an eyebrow. "Really?"

Madeline grinned.

CHAPTER 14

Madeline glided down the long corridor to the bed chamber. She had to stop herself from breaking out into a dance. Not only she had gotten the antidote, but she had also found a solution to Moira's five-hundred-year-old problem—and without the need of super soldiers.

The electronic door to the room slid open to reveal Ciaran sitting in the armchair, his eyes narrowed. "What in God's name happened to your face?" he snapped.

She felt a faint female sense in the room, hovering in the air. She couldn't figure out whose it was. She just knew it was female. Madeline wiped at the drop of blood on her split lip. "A mild altercation."

"If I hadn't snapped out of the drug's effects, would you have told me where you had gone, or would you simply have climbed back into bed and pretended you hadn't drugged me?"

"I don't think you snapped out of the drug on your own."

"I did."

"Who was she? The person who peeled the drug off?"

"What are you implying?"

"I'm asking for the facts. Who was she?"

Ciaran held up the drug pad. "It fell off by itself."

"Not possible."

"It's not relevant and certainly not important."

"So what is then?"

Ciaran stood and approached Madeline. "Where have you been? What did you do? You left your wrist unit, so I couldn't track you, but I'm sure I can track the vehicle you used."

"Track me? Like I'm a piece of your data? Why don't you tell me who the woman was? Or don't you want me to know?"

"You're being unreasonable, Madeline. There was no woman here."

"Then let's check the surveillance."

"Do you know what it felt like to wake up to find that you were gone? If you had plans, all you had to do is tell me. You didn't have to drug me and go behind my back," Ciaran snarled.

The look of anger and annoyance in his eyes slashed at her heart. "There *was* a woman. I can feel her. I can sense her. And now I can see her in your mind," Madeline retorted.

Ciaran waved his arms in the air. "Now, I'm at fault. And all because of an imaginative woman." He strode to the control panel and punched the activate button. "You want to see the surveillance? Let's see it. Then you will tell me where you've been . . ." He trailed off.

On the screen, Sizx entered the residence, bypassing the security. She punched in a code on the lock and entered the bedroom. She peeled the drug pad from Ciaran's neck, kissed his face, and left before he awakened. She wiped the security trail at the entrance but forgot about the log in the bedroom wing.

Ciaran looked at Madeline and saw her raised eyebrow. "She was just trying to help." Ciaran shoved his hands into his pockets.

"She woke you, kissed you, and came back to pick me up." Madeline laughed, wincing from the slight pain in her broken lip.

"Picked you up from where?"

"Oh, don't you turn this around on me. There's more to her than meets the eye. She wants to do a lot more than kiss you."

"It was out of my control, wasn't it? Since when did you turn into a jealous shrew?"

"I can't afford to be jealous, Ciaran. Otherwise, I'd spend my entire life fighting off the women who swarm around you like bees to honey."

"You're saying I intentionally attract those women?"

"Do you like her?"

"Madeline!"

She nodded. "So you do have feelings for her."

"I . . ."

Madeline threw her hands in the air and turned on her heel.

"Don't you walk out on me," Ciaran snarled.

Madeline turned back and stared at him. "Ciaran LeBlanc, you've gotten too used to people doing whatever you say. Find someone else to boss around. I'm leaving." She turned to the door.

"There's a lot to do. We have a universe we're responsible for. I only have five days. Can you prioritize those items a little higher than your little snit?"

"My little *snit!*" She approached Ciaran, jabbing her finger at his chest. "For your information, while you were sleeping—and being kissed by another woman—I was negotiating with Moira. I have your antidote. So you will have more than five days to live—unless you want to cut your life short on your own. I've saved your ass. And I'm sorry if my negotiation hurt your galactic-sized ego."

She slammed the antidote patch on the table, shoved him backward, and walked out of the room. From the corridor, she heard something smash.

At the entrance of the residence, Sizx sauntered in. Before she could greet Madeline, Madeline gave her a knuckle punch in the face. Sizx reeled back outside.

"If you had meant to wipe the logs, you shouldn't have left the one in the bedroom," Madeline growled.

Sizx rubbed at her jaw. Her eyes filled with concern. "How's Ciaran?" she asked, running into the hallway and passing Tadgh, who was on his way in.

Madeline raised her arms in the air, talking to Tadgh. "Is that woman for real? Should I offer her a chance to sleep with my husband?"

"What?" Tadgh asked, totally confused.

At the end of the hallway, Sizx ran straight into Ciaran. He pushed her aside and called out, "Madeline!"

"Don't follow me," she grunted and bolted for the door.

It was Sizx, not just any woman. She had seen Ciaran's eyes twinkle with intrigue the first time they met. Sizx had many things she didn't. Perfect looks. Technological literacy. The ability to take orders and directions from Ciaran without question. She was not impulsive. And Ciaran would never call *her* a snit!

***

Storming into an empty capsule parked at the platform, Madeline pressed her palm to the verificator to activate the vehicle. The capsule shuddered and awakened. The control panel flashed questions about the destination. Madeline entered Sciphil One residence. The machine declared her command invalid. She tried other commands. The machine kept spitting out rejections. Tears poured down her face. She pounded at all the buttons and pulled her dagger to stab the recalcitrant machine. A robotic voice warned about consequences for vandalism.

"May I come in?" Ciaran's voice came from the door of the capsule.

Madeline looked. He stood there, hands in his pockets, penitent, awaiting her permission to enter. She nodded and moved away from the control panel.

"I can take you to Sciphil One residence," he offered.

"No need."

He tilted her face and looked into her eyes. He wiped away her tears. "I'm sorry I caused you pain."

She looked at him, thinking he probably felt as much pain as she did. "I need some time by myself."

"Understood." He nodded. "Please stay." Then he looked at her.

She could never resist that look, so she looked away. "I can't . . . I just . . ."

"Okay. You don't have to explain." He programmed the capsule for her. "Will you send me a message when you arrive so I know you're safe?"

She nodded. He tilted her face again and lightly kissed the dimple on her left cheek. "I love you," he whispered. He gazed at her for a moment and then stepped out of the capsule.

The capsule lifted, hovered for a moment, and then zoomed out of the station. In the capsule's mirror, she could see Ciaran standing on the platform like a king in a lonely castle. *Where was she going? To her residence—where she'd be a lonely queen in her own castle.*

CHAPTER 15

The computer monitor had settled into sleeping mode as he hadn't touched it for a long time. The Master smiled to himself. He had gotten more information about Ciaran than he had hoped for. He closed his eyes, imagining the day he would gloriously become the king of Eudaiz.

His plan wasn't ideal. But it was as good as it got. He heard a faint sound behind him. He had sent his everyone away. This location was very discreet, and his magic protected it from ordinary eyes. As he turned around to see what had made the noise, a cloud of blackness flew at him.

It was too fast for him to figure out what he was dealing with, and then his whole world plunged into darkness.

***

"Ciaran!"

Ciaran turned toward Tadgh, who was calling him at the entrance to the capsule platform.

"What was that all about?" Tadgh asked.

Ciaran shook his head. "You're here about Jo, I guess. We don't have much time left before we have to officiate her as Sciphil Four."

"I can't find her!" Tadgh exclaimed.

"But you live with her. In the same residence!"

"I promised Ayana I'd convince Jo to take Sciphil Four position instead of Five. And I did. But we had a disagreement. She left, and when I called her . . . there were no signals on her communicator. And I sensed Kyle close by."

Ciaran shook his head and headed inside toward the control room.

There, the computer screen flashed. A blue dot tracking the communicator in Jo's wrist unit blinked at them. "That's the border of District Six," Ciaran muttered.

"What's she doing there?"

"I don't think it's Jo. It's her unit. She must have dropped it. There have been a couple of times when I was sucked into unstable dimensional holes from other universes and came out on the outskirts of District Six."

"So she's either left or been captured and taken to another universe via one of those holes?" Tadgh asked.

Ciaran nodded. "Let's see who has her," he said and search for visual surveillance data. The footage on the screen showed Jo being carried out of a capsule. She wasn't conscious. Her kidnappers were invisible. Her wrist unit dropped on the ground before she vanished into the dimensional hole.

"What creatures are those? Why are they invisible?" Tadgh asked.

Ciaran shook his head. "They're Xiilok creatures, and they're only invisible to machines. We can see them."

"Xiilok?"

"I'll explain to you on the way. We can't use ordinary soldiers, so we'll have to go there and get her back. You have your sword with you?" Ciaran asked as he strode to the door.

CHAPTER 16

At the entrance to Xiilok, Tadgh stomped his feet on the spongy ground. "This is totally weird," he mumbled. Then he pointed at the well. "That's the well you mentioned?"

Ciaran nodded. It was the well located next to the large black tree with red leaves, bearing the Greek symbol for "drink." When Ciaran had come here with Madeline, they'd thought it was the Xiilok way of welcoming visitors. But now, Ciaran deduced that the water in the well turned people into Xiilok citizens. He wasn't sure what it did to those who imbibed socially, but he was sure that it had something to do with their worm-filled irises and the fact that they turned into worm puddles when killed. Maybe the advantage they had was that they could see the shifted dimensions in Xiilok and in the Daimon Gate. The only thing Ciaran and Tadgh had to rely on now was their technology.

"I'm sure if we don't drink the water here, we're not going to miss out on anything," Ciaran muttered, tapping on the liquid map. The screen swirled and then sat still, revealing nothing.

"Great technology. I think my eyes will work better than that contraption," Tadgh said.

"This place is full of dimensional gateways and traps. It's totally built on illusion. If you drop into one of those oblivion holes, don't ask me to come to your rescue, Tadgh. Now stay still, will you?"

A group of four men, led by Nick in his leather jacket and cowboy boots, appeared from a dimensional doorway. It was as if they had appeared out of thin air.

"Holy cow!" Tadgh gasped.

"You're late," Ciaran said. He noted that the group had four men now, instead of five. Nick appeared to be the leader. Something in him had changed in a short period of time.

Nick's grin slanted. "According to my time, we're not late. What do you want this time?"

"We're looking for a girl in her late twenties. Petite, big green eyes, foxy face, long black hair, very pretty," Ciaran said. Tadgh seemed surprised by his brother's detailed description of Jo.

Nick had stopped smiling now. He glanced at the other members of his group. They gathered and spoke in a strange language, breaking out in some kind of debate. Then three of the men walked away, abandoning Nick. Nick watched his friends disappear into another dimension, and then he turned around to face Ciaran and Tadgh.

"This job is going to cost you."

"Naturally." Tadgh's sarcasm was palpable.

"There are plenty of us in Xiilok. Why me?" Nick asked.

"I'm a good judge of character. Out of those I hired for the zombie job, you were the only one who left your money in London. You have vision," Ciaran explained. "How do I know you have reliable info? I don't care to be strung along by an outlaw."

Nick sneered. "As if . . ." He paused. "Hey, I know who you are. King of Eudaiz, right?"

Ciaran arched an eyebrow.

"I'll take that as a yes," Nick said. "I don't want your money for this one."

Tadgh frowned and shifted his right shoulder to give his weapon arm some flexibility—just in case he had to make a move.

Ciaran smiled at his brother's reaction. "What do you want in exchange for the information?" Ciaran asked.

"I want to join Eudaiz. I want to become a citizen."

Ciaran cleared his throat. "What do you know about Eudaiz?"

"It's a place of purity and true happiness. I know it's unlikely for us to get in, but since you're the king, you ought to have the authority to make an exception."

Ciaran nodded. "I don't have time to explain to you now. I could give you a false promise to keep your hopes up and bide our time, but as you said, purity is the main makeup of Eudaizian citizens, and as their leader, hustling my way through this wouldn't be a good example. So let me say this—I am requesting the information in order to rescue a friend of ours. And if this mission is successful, I promise you that I will talk to my council and consider you for a position within our guards."

Nick contemplated and nodded.

"It's a deal," he said.

"What about your group?" Tadgh asked. "Will they leak the fact that we're here?"

Nick shook his head. "They're decent guys. They won't do the job for you this time, but I don't think they'd betray me."

"You're overconfident, Nick," Ciaran said.

Nick smirked. "No need to stress. When I said we have a deal, I meant it. We're Xiilok fighters, but we do have our standards."

"So you're willing to work for us only with Ciaran's promise that we will speak to the council about your citizenship. You understand that there's no guarantee, right?" Tadgh asked.

Nick nodded.

"If this is a trap, if anything happens to either of us, the entire council of Eudaiz, the committee of the Daimon Gate and all nine thousand of their gatekeepers, all committees of participating universes, and thousands of skillful, resourceful, and important people working for us on Earth will hunt you down," Ciaran warned.

Nick shrugged. "It's only me. Why are you so worried? I'm ready when you are." He turned around and started walking. Ciaran signaled Tadgh. They followed with caution.

CHAPTER 17

Nick crouched against a large tree trunk surrounded by rocks. Ciaran and Tadgh did the same. Ciaran knew that Nick could see the dimensional gates and traps and could tell the difference between real and illusional objects in Xiilok. Ciaran and Tadgh shadowed his exact footsteps and actions.

Nick directed their attention to two pointy stones that formed a small, arched doorway. "Those who live in Xiilok but are not one of us live in places marked by these stone doors."

"What do you mean 'one of you'?" Tadgh asked.

"If you drink the water in the well, you become one of the Xiiloks. We can see everything here as it really is. You outlanders can't see much, so you tend to die by falling into traps and oblivion holes. That's how being a Xiilok protects us. It's a dangerous place for a non-Xiilok to live."

"You're saying that whoever captured our friend is non-Xiilok? And he's as blind as we are in terms of the dimensional gates and traps around here?" Ciaran asked.

Nick nodded. "We don't touch the outsiders living behind those gates because they tend to bring jobs to the fighters. If I killed him, I would upset those who live out of his pocket."

"Who is he?" Tadgh asked.

Nick shrugged. "Don't know and don't care."

"What weapon works best here?" Ciaran asked.

"The most primitive ones. Like those you carry now. Knives, swords, daggers. I can't explain why, but anything using technology and complicated physical mechanisms won't work. When I first came, I had a rifle. When I fired, the bullet went sideways—nearly killed my friend."

Ciaran nodded.

The door slid open. A group of men with hoods covering their faces walked out. They followed a Xiilok creature, working as a guide.

Once they were out of eyeshot, Ciaran said, "We're going in now, Tadgh." Tadgh nodded. They darted between the rocks, moving closer to the door. Nick ran after Tadgh. "What are you doing, Nick?" Ciaran asked.

"I'm getting you inside the compound. You're blind as bats here. You think you can get through the door without being able to see it?"

Ciaran nodded and stepped aside to allow Nick to lead.

Nick ran along what looked to Tadgh and Ciaran to be a treeline. He ducked down a couple of times, and Ciaran and Tadgh did exactly the same. He seemed to be turning a corner and turned to speak, but before he could utter a word, Tadgh hit his head on something.

"Fuck me!" Tadgh yelped and grabbed his forehead. He was a couple of inches taller than Nick. Ciaran was a bit taller than Tadgh, and he bent down especially low to avoid a collision with the invisible object. Nick chuckled.

"That's the back door. What does it look like to you?" Nick pointed to something in the distance.

"A large rock," Tadgh said.

Nick shrugged. "Well, it's a door. When you get inside, you'll be able to see normally."

"Thanks," Ciaran said and led the way. He pushed at the large rock. It slid open, revealing a long dark hallway. He stepped in, and Tadgh followed.

The long hallway was lit by a dim green light from illuminated rocks. Ciaran and Tadgh moved quickly along the edge of the rock wall. The two brothers were stealthy and agile, moving like leopards. They heard the faint echo of footsteps. They turned and hid behind a large rock column. If no technology worked here, Ciaran thought, then it would have to be hand-to-hand combat, which he preferred.

A group of five fighters walked past. They glanced down the corridor and then kept moving.

"If they're guards, remind me never hire them in the future," Ciaran whispered.

"I don't think they have a future anyway." Tadgh smiled and darted silently toward the group from behind.

"Hey!" Tadgh called out. The five turned around, but before they could make a sound, his daggers sliced the throats of two of the fighters.

"I'm here!" Ciaran said from the back. The three remaining fighters turned around. Ciaran swung his daggers and cut down two in mere seconds. The last man standing drew his sword, but Tadgh knocked it out of his hand from behind and pressed his own dagger against the fighter's throat.

"You're not a good fighter, but you're wise enough to know what I'll do to you if you make a sound," Tadgh said, pressing his dagger harder into his flesh. A stream of blood running down his neck, the fighter raised his arms, surrendering.

"Take us to where the girl from Eudaiz is kept."

"I . . ."

Tadgh applied even more pressure.

"All right! Don't kill me! All right!"

He led the way to a basement. Tadgh kept his dagger at the fighter's back. "Open the door." The fighter obeyed. Tadgh spun him around and pushed him toward Ciaran. Ciaran grabbed him, using his dagger to control him.

Tadgh pushed the door open and walked in. A silver tray flew at him, followed by a torrent of unidentifiable objects.

"The next time you walk in here, I'll have daggers flying at you," Jo's voice shrieked out from a corner of the dimly lit room. Tadgh blocked the flying objects the best he could, cursing when some of them crashed into his body. Ciaran wanted to help, but he couldn't abandon the fighter.

"Tadgh!" Jo whispered when she heard his curses.

"Be careful, Tadgh. We don't know who's who. She's been captured. She might have been turned. Like Libby," Ciaran said from the outside. He dragged the fighter into the room with him.

"Light the room up," Ciaran said to the fighter.

"Ciaran!" Jo called out. "Ciaran, is that you?"

"I can't. You need a light rock," the fighter cried out as Ciaran's dagger pierced his neck.

Jo charged at Tadgh.

"No touching, Tadgh. We don't know who she is yet," Ciaran called out. He could see Jo's silhouette stop.

"What are you talking about, Ciaran?" Jo asked. "Tadgh? Are you there?" Tadgh withdrew. Jo could see his shadow taking steps backward.

"Okay, lady, we're not sure if you're Jo or not. It's too dark, and there's no time to find a light. You're going to have to follow us to the corridor. We have to leave right now," Ciaran said, dragging his quarry back outside the room. Having no technology worked to their advantage—there was no alarm or electronic surveillance anywhere.

They returned to the long, empty corridor which led to the back door. The dead bodies of the fighters had long since turned to worm-infested puddles.

In the corridor, Jo and Tadgh stared at each other. Tadgh felt every inch of his body quiver. The woman in front of him looked like Jo. But he couldn't forget the feeling of the spear she had put through his heart. Jo advanced, and Tadgh stepped backward.

"Stop," Tadgh said.

"Stop right there, Jo," Ciaran stated firmly. "One step closer to my brother, and I might have to use my dagger on you. Black Rock and Xiilok creatures can take many forms. We need to make sure you are who you really are. We need to know they haven't turned you."

Tears filled Jo's eyes. She nodded.

Ciaran swung the handle of his dagger at the fighter's head and knocked him unconscious. He dropped to the floor like a felled tree. Ciaran then approached Jo. "Look at me, Jo."

Jo turned around. Ciaran lifted her chin, tilted her head back, and looked deeply into her irises. He saw two huge green eyes. He saw Jo's face. But Ciaran didn't have Madeline's instinct. Jo was not a Xiilok, but she could still be a Black Rock creature. She didn't have the hollow voice that the Black Rock creatures did, but Ciaran didn't trust himself enough to draw any conclusions.

Jo's lip trembled. But she didn't cry.

"It's Jo. It's her, Ciaran. Can't you tell?" Tadgh exclaimed.

"No, I can't," Ciaran said. The scene when Jo had stabbed Tadgh through the heart in the Daimon Gate was still too raw for Ciaran to believe anything for sure. It hadn't been Jo—it was a Black Rock creature in disguise. But the memory of it still haunted Ciaran's nightmares.

Jo cried. Tadgh grabbed her and embraced her.

"No, Tadgh." Ciaran grabbed his brother, but Tadgh pushed him away.

"How can you be so cold, Ciaran?" Tadgh criticized.

"Because I don't want to see you die again."

"And *you've* never done that? How many times have you died in front of Madeline?"

Jo released Tadgh. She brushed her fingers across the scar. Then she spoke to Ciaran, "How can

I prove I'm not a Black Rock creature? How can I know for myself?"

Ciaran looked into Tadgh's eyes. "Only Madeline can tell. All I know is that Black Rock creatures turn into black puddles when they die and evaporate into nothingness. And they don't bleed."

Jo grabbed Tadgh's dagger and pushed him away. She slashed into her arm. Ciaran stared at the stream of blood.

"How much blood do you want?" Jo asked.

Tadgh tried to grab her. She withdrew. "How much blood do you need to believe, Ciaran?" she repeated.

Ciaran had no idea. He had been so wrong in his judgment in this universe. He felt for Jo. He wanted to believe her. But he just could not forget the spear piercing Tadgh's heart.

Jo slashed one more time at her arm.

"Jo!" Tadgh yelled out.

"How much blood, Ciaran? Or do you have to kill me to be sure?" Jo asked.

"That's enough. I believe you," Ciaran said. Jo dropped the dagger. Tadgh pulled her into his arms. Ciaran saw the resentment in Tadgh's eyes, but he brushed it off. He'd seen that look before from his brother. Ciaran turned. "We have to leave now. You can continue that when we're safe and sound in Eudaiz."

Footsteps echoed. Ciaran glanced down the corridor to see approaching troops. "I was so sure this was a trap," he said. They turned and ran toward the back door. Fighters poured into the corridor now. The three of them exited, and Tadgh handed Jo one of his daggers.

CHAPTER 18

"This way!" Nick called and waved and pointed to the right. Tadgh held Jo's hand and went to the right. Ciaran jammed the door and followed.

"Duck," Nick yelled, but not before Tadgh hit his head again.

"Damn it!" Tadgh cursed.

Ciaran charged forward. "Follow me," he said. They ran after Nick as fast as they could. The fighters had broken out of the back door and pursued them.

Nick stopped and pointed. "If we cross this creek, they won't follow us. On the other side, there's a group of non-Xiiloks. I don't know them, but I'm told they're nasty pieces of shit. If we kill them, this way becomes a shortcut to Daimon Gate."

"And the other way?" Ciaran asked, looking back. The fighters still stormed out of the compound, swarming toward them like ants. "Forget I asked," Ciaran muttered and looked again at the creek.

Nick frowned. "The non-Xiilok on the other side are nasty creatures, but at least there are only a handful of them. The water in the creek runs fast, but it's not deep. Just follow me." Nick led, but Ciaran paused.

"What do you see where the creek is?" Nick asked.

"I see the creek," Tadgh said.

"Me, too," Jo confirmed.

Ciaran said nothing. What he saw was a sea of maggots. He was sure it was an illusion, and he knew it targeted him.

"Ciaran, don't you swim?" Nick asked.

"What?"

"You seem scared of the water. If you're seeing something else, the other two can assure you that it's only shallow water you're stepping into."

"Of course, it's water," Ciaran grumbled and darted toward the creek. It was cold. He focused on swimming to the other side. Tadgh followed.

On the other side of the creek, an awful and familiar aura engulfed Ciaran. He couldn't make sense of it. He couldn't seem to focus, but he tried. Everything was blurry, and the air seemed to spin. Ciaran looked down to be sure his body wasn't swaying. He concentrated again. When had he felt this way before? A strange noise echoed in his mind. Lyla's scream. He had experienced the same nauseated feeling at Orla castle when something had tried to pry information out of his head.

Hell, he wouldn't let it happen, Ciaran thought. *Focus!* he told himself.

They heard howling noises. A bunch of wolves emerged from the woods and encircled them. Gigantic, menacing wolves unlike any they had encountered before. These wolves weren't computer-simulated, neither were they ordinary wolves like those they'd fought in the Daimon Gate. These animals were here for a purpose. Ciaran narrowed his eyes. They were hunting for a trophy—his mind.

"I ...I thought the non-Xiilok were human. I hate dogs," Nick stuttered.

Ciaran glanced around. Six gray wolves lurked, teeth bared.

"Could you stick around to show my brother the way out?" Ciaran asked Nick.

"Do I have a choice?"

Ciaran glanced across the creek and saw the opposite bank blanketed with Xiilok fighters. He looked back at the gray wolves. An excruciating pain pounded in his head. He knew it was the same as what he had experienced at Orla castle. Something was prying information out of his head. But these wolves were a real and present danger. Ciaran couldn't even ask Tadgh to knock him out because if he was unconscious, he would slow the group down.

"Tadgh!" Ciaran called out.

"What?" Tadgh approached. "Your nose is bleeding, Ciaran."

Ciaran wiped the blood off. "When you get a chance, follow Nick. He knows where the gateway is."

"You want me to leave you here?"

"Something—or someone—is trying to get into my head. It happened before. Just like what Kyle did to you. But whatever this is, I can't control it."

"You're not going to do anything stupid, are you?"

Ciaran looked at his brother. "If anything happens to me, promise me you'll watch over Madeline and my kids."

"Now you're talking nonsense." Tadgh shook his head.

"Just promise me," Ciaran stressed as a sharp pain cut through his mind. He staggered and clutched his head.

"I'll knock you out," Tadgh said. But before he could do so, a wolf charged him and knocked him to the ground. Ciaran pulled his daggers and pierced the wolf's head. It howled as its blood and brains poured out and rained down on Tadgh.

"It won't let you knock me out. I'll do my best before I have to turn the knife on myself," Ciaran said, gripping the second wolf. Tadgh jumped to his feet, slashing at the third wolf. The wolves were in attack mode. Jo stabbed at the one attacking her. Nick killed one that bit his leg.

They fought and withdrew toward where Nick suggested the gateway was. The wolves kept coming. Ciaran knew they wouldn't last long. Even if they reached the Daimon Gate, the thing trying to rip the memories out of his mind would follow them through.

The pain in his head was staggering. He could hardly hold on to his daggers. From the corner of his eyes, Ciaran saw a shadow. He left the group and charged toward it. Behind a large tree stood an eight-foot man wearing a long black robe. Ciaran swung his daggers, stabbing at the man. The man stepped back, and Ciaran saw he wasn't eight feet tall at all—he hovered in the air, and his feet didn't touch the ground. The man had an ancient face and may have been good-looking in his time. But at the moment, he looked like death.

"You're the one who wants something from me," Ciaran said.

The man croaked, "Give me the spell. Tell me what it is." His voice was hollow, echoing up from hell. He reached his hands out and lifted Ciaran. Ciaran dropped his daggers. His head pounded, and his nose bled. But he wouldn't let his memories go. He shut his mind down as much as he could.

"Give me the spell," the ancient creature repeated.

Tadgh stabbed him from behind, and he dropped Ciaran to the ground and swung his arm to throw Tadgh away. Blood poured from the man's wound, black and gelatinous like jelly. Tadgh noticed the man still hovered above the ground. He charged him again with his dagger. The man lifted his arms, raising Tadgh from the ground from a distance. Unseen hands choked Tadgh. Tadgh tried to break free but couldn't.

Lying on the ground, his mind and body numb, Ciaran knew it wouldn't be long until his brother was dead. No matter how much Jo and Nick attacked the man, he wouldn't go down. He wanted the spell from Ciaran. All Ciaran had to do was release control of his mind. He had to take care of his brother. It was the least he could do. He closed his eyes and willed himself to let go.

As soon as Ciaran relaxed his control, the man let Tadgh go. He stretched his invisible arms toward Ciaran, and Ciaran's body was lifted from the ground. His head lolled. He felt a hot surge of energy and then something suctioning his life force.

Ciaran let go of the information the man had asked for. For a long moment, he felt nothing but darkness.

Ciaran opened his eyes to Tadgh, who was shaking his shoulders like a crazed man. The trees in the background swayed and spun. Ciaran closed his eyes and reopened them. The world was still spinning. He felt empty, drained.

"Okay, up brother. Let's get you out of here." Tadgh sat Ciaran up. Nick took the other shoulder. Together, they hauled Ciaran off the ground. "There you go. One step at a time. Just like a baby," Tadgh said.

Ciaran stood. He pushed Tadgh and Nick away and grabbed his head. It wasn't lack of energy. He had enough strength to fight another round with the wolves. It was the hollow pain in his head—so unbearable that it blinded him. "Where's the man?" Ciaran asked.

"Vanished. Ran away like a lunatic. And he looked happy, too." Jo said.

"I can walk by myself. I don't need you," Ciaran said and walked away aimlessly.

Nick charged to the front of the group. "Follow me then."

Tadgh grabbed Jo's hand and walked alongside Ciaran.

They passed the gateway to the Daimon Gate. Ciaran could feel Tadgh's hand steering his back when he veered the wrong way or was about to slam into a hard object. He couldn't think straight. His vision was blurred, and he felt as if his head was on fire and his brain matter was oozing, waiting for a chance to explode through his ears.

"Ciaran!" Tadgh called out. No response from Ciaran. "Ciaran!" Tadgh repeated.

"What?"

"We're inside the Daimon Gate. Are we going straight to the Host residence?"

"No." Ciaran shook his head. That was all he could come up with right now. "No," he repeated. He knew he had to do better than this. He knew there were many things he had to do before heading to Eudaiz, but he couldn't articulate them. Aside from the excruciating pain, there was nothing else in his mind right now. Everything burned inside him.

"Ciaran, we're going to the Host's residence. When we get there, I'm going to call Madeline. Only she can fix you," Tadgh persisted.

"No," Ciaran grunted out the word. He squeezed his eyes shut, hoping to concentrate more on his thoughts. "Orla castle . . . we need to go there . . ." He pulled out the electronic map Jennifer had given him. He couldn't see where Jo was standing, so he just held the pad out.

"Here's the map, Jo," Ciaran said.

Jo took the pad from him. She was a tech genius, and he wouldn't have to explain to her how to use the map. Something lingered at the back of his head about the reason they couldn't go to the Host residence. He remembered it now—Nick was with them. Nick had helped them, and they had a deal. But he still didn't know Nick, and there was no way he would let him near the residence where his parents and children were living.

Jo led with the map.

"Tadgh," Ciaran called out.

"Yes."

"We need to go to Lorcan and Orla, let Nick stay with them, and then head straight to Eudaiz. Even though the time in the Daimon Gate and that in Eudaiz are different, I know we're running late for Jo's officiation." His vision started to blur, and he shook his head to pull himself together.

"Okay. Why don't I take Nick to Lorcan and Orla? You take Jo straight to Tower Four," Tadgh said.

"I need to get to the computer now to do some research on the ennead code," Ciaran said and strode ahead. He knew he couldn't handle a computer now. He needed Lorcan's help. They could get to Tower Four, and Jo had the skill to help him, but she would be in the officiation chamber.

Ciaran couldn't see a goddamn thing. He felt Tadgh's hand on his back, pushing and guiding him. Because he couldn't see much himself, he willingly followed his brother's guidance.

CHAPTER 19

In Sciphil One residence, Madeline scrambled up from the floor. She must have passed out again. The precognition had hit her hard. In her mind, she saw Tower Four crumbled to the ground. Ciaran, Tadgh, and Jo were inside the tower when it was collapsing. They must have failed the Sciphil Four officiation. And it wasn't just the tower that would collapse—Ayana had told them that failure to officiate a Sciphil would crumble the entire Eudaiz energy system and destroy it completely.

More than six hundred billion lives.

What had they done?

Now she understood Ciaran better than ever—his vision, his resistance to give Moira access to super soldiers. Actions that had implications for galactic consequences had to be considered with care and should never be driven purely by personal reasons. Ciaran put the interest of the multiverse above all personal matters.

He didn't want that kind of responsibility on his shoulders. He loved her, and all he wanted was his family. But this journey had taken them down this path, and their lives were not their own anymore.

To that extent, he was right . . . she was really a petulant and impulsive snit!

***

The door to Orla castle slid open, revealing Lorcan and Orla. Orla frowned at Ciaran's pale face and the distant look in his eyes. Jo shrieked in joy when she saw Lorcan and Orla. She flew to them, giving them both bear hugs. Tadgh was flabbergasted.

"These two rescued me from Zen in London," Jo said.

Tadgh nodded. "That explains why you weren't in the car at Rufford Abbey." Tadgh recalled the incident vividly. Zen had kidnapped Jo from New York and blackmailed Madeline to go to London for a rescue. Madeline and Ciaran had attempted a rescue at Rufford Abbey, killing Zen only to discover that Jo wasn't there. Tadgh couldn't recall much after the bomb exploded in Zen's car while Tadgh was standing nearby.

"And that's how you know so much about us. You must have been following us all around London," Ciaran said.

"Rescuing Jo was our last job on Earth," Lorcan said.

"I sure hope so," Orla added. "You must be Tadgh?"

Tadgh nodded. "This is Nick, from Xiilok."

Orla glanced at Nick's irises. "Naturally," she said.

"We need your help," Ciaran said, pausing as a sharp pain sliced through his mind. He winced.

"Come on in," Lorcan said.

Tadgh steered Ciaran in the direction of the hallway.

"We need to use your computer system. We're in a hurry," Ciaran continued.

Lorcan nodded and turned into the computer room. Outside the room, he paused. "I can only take Ciaran." Everyone stopped, and Ciaran proceeded into the room with Lorcan. He could see the blurry edges of computers and tables and Lorcan moving. The pain throbbed in his head. Ciaran knew there was no way he could operate a computer right now.

"Could you help me do a search?" Ciaran asked.

"Sure," Lorcan said and activated the computer.

"I need an algorithm to calculate the possibilities of . . ." Ciaran shook his head, trying to clear the pain. He drew in a deep breath. "If you enter ennead, the names of nine gods in Egyptian mythology, adding a variation of . . . damn it!" Ciaran grunted as the sharp pain stabbed at his brain.

"You look like you're about to die, Ciaran."

"Can I have a moment to myself? I won't touch your computers."

"Of course." Lorcan glanced at Ciaran's face then left the room.

Outside, everyone watched the monitor of the surveillance camera Orla had turned on. On the screen, Ciaran grabbed his head as if in excruciating pain. He leaned against the wall, sliding to the floor.

"I have to call Madeline," Tadgh said.

"What can she do?" Orla asked.

"I don't know. But she can always fix him. Whenever shit happens, she fixes it."

"Not this time. Tell me what happened in Xiilok," Orla demanded.

"Who are you? What do you know?" Tadgh asked.

"Orla knows things that you don't. You can call Madeline. But I'm afraid it might be too late," Lorcan said.

They looked at the screen. Ciaran stood and punched at the wall until his knuckles bled. It apparently didn't help. He slid to the floor again.

***

Ciaran's mind was burning. He felt as if his soul was melting. He needed Madeline. He needed to see her, to talk to her, to touch her. He thought of his children and the family he hadn't had a chance yet to cherish. He knew he was going to die shortly. The thought of dying without seeing Madeline again burned him more than the fire in his mind.

He hadn't taken the antidote she had gotten from Moira. The poison must have accelerated after the incident in Xiilok. It was unstoppable now. He didn't regret his decision, but he needed to see his wife again.

Then he sensed her. Amid the blinding haze of pain and hallucination, he felt his mate. The sensation was primal. It was urgent. She came. She touched his shoulders. "Ciaran," she said gently.

"Madeline." He pulled his wife into his arms and kissed her.

"Easy, easy, darling," she said. "Look at me."

Ciaran's eyes glazed over. He couldn't see a thing. He could only feel her, touch her, and hear her voice. The foreign object on his shoulders that he used to call his head was not working. He couldn't think.

She tucked a strand of hair away from his face. He tried to kiss her again. She held his face and said, "Ciaran, you're in pain. Tell me what happened."

"I don't know."

"You always know. Whatever was in Xiilok tried to get to you, didn't it? What was it? A man? A woman?"

"I don't know. I couldn't feel anything. I'm going to die soon, Madeline. I just want to tell you I'm sorry for what happened between us. I didn't mean to call you names. There has never been any woman—or anyone at all—between us. There will never be . . ."

"I know, Ciaran." She cupped his face. "Tell me what happened in Xiilok."

"No, no. You don't understand. I didn't take the antidote you gave me. I am not against what you did . . . I just . . ." The strength rushed out of him. The ground beneath him seemed to move. He almost fell onto Madeline.

She propped him up. "So it's the poison that's hurting you. Let me fix it." She pressed her thumbs gently on his temples and moved them in circles. His body started to sway.

"You can't fix poison, Madeline. I can't save Eudaiz . . . I'm sorry . . . I love you . . . I love our children . . . I wish . . . things had turned out differently . . ."

"Listen to me," she continued gently. "You're in pain. Let me help you out with this, and then we can have a proper conversation."

"We won't make it. I'm sorry. I can't make it."

"Yes, you can, Ciaran. Let me help you. Just say yes for me. Please?" She continued to rub his temples.

"Yes."

"What did it want from you? The person in Xiilok."

He shook his head, trying to stay awake.

She whispered, "Come on darling. Tell me. Please."

His world spun. "It wanted the spell Lyla gave me." He tried to grab Madeline.

She held him. "So there was magic. Okay. Did you tell it what it wanted to know?"

"I don't know. I don't remember."

"Try. Do it for me. You remember, don't you? You can tell me. Did you let go of the spell? Let it out, darling. Tell me." She embraced him now. Her voice was soothing.

His world spun out of orbit. The ground below him caved in. The walls whirled, distorted, and blurred out of their frames. "Yes, I did . . . I did . . . I let it get the spell," Ciaran whispered. His eyes rolled back. He collapsed.

***

"Ayana, we're in serious trouble. You need to come and get me at once at Sciphil One residence," Madeline shouted to the communication panel.

On the screen, Ayana stared at her, "Where's Ciaran? Tadgh is supposed to be with Jo. Ciaran should be with them at Tower Four right now. I saw all the energy channels for the officiation engaged."

"It might look like they're there, but they're not. I know they're not there. Trust me. Could you come and get me? I can't control this stupid flying machine."

Ayana nodded. "Right away."

CHAPTER 20

Ciaran scrambled back up to his feet. He didn't quite get his balance, so he staggered and grabbed at something that looked like a standing monitor on a table. He felt hands holding his shoulders up before be crashed onto the table. "Easy, brother."

Ciaran shook his head to clear his mind. The haze was still there. The pain was still lingering but manageable. Tadgh was holding him. *Madeline?* He looked around. He was in the computer lab at Orla castle. Lorcan, Orla, Nick, Tadgh, and Jo were there. But there was no sign of Madeline.

His gaze stopped on Orla's face. He knew what she had done. "Thank you," Ciaran said.

Orla nodded. "You might not care for my approach. But there was poison in your body and traces of magic practiced on your mind. The combination should have killed you. Consider the magic part handled. But regarding the poison, I can only help ease the pain so you can do whatever it is you have to do."

"That's good enough. Thank you again," Ciaran said. "Tadgh, based on how long we've been here, can you calculate the time in Eudaiz now?"

"Yes, but it will take me a bit. My gut feeling is we should have been at Tower Four a while ago."

"Then what are we waiting for?" Ciaran raced out of the room, followed by everyone. "You stay here, Nick. I'll come back for you later," he said before jumping into a hovering capsule parked outside the castle. The capsule zoomed away.

"You're welcome!" Lorcan muttered.

***

The capsule landed in front of Tower Four. Ciaran, Tadgh, and Jo jumped right out and raced toward the gate. The imposing structure of the gigantic tower peered down on them, waiting. From the corner of his eye, Ciaran saw the flash of an incoming capsule. A rail-free individual capsule landed, and from inside, Madeline and Ayana rushed out.

The sight of Madeline rattled him. He shuddered, thinking about the moment he was dying in the lab when he thought he would never see his wife again. But there was no time for sentiment at the moment.

Ciaran ran toward the control panel of the tower, verified himself, and entered passes for everyone.

The gigantic round structure shuddered. Its nine layers of thick steel and concrete shuddered and slid open to reveal a narrow pathway. It closed as soon as the last person stepped in.

Inside the tower, the hallway opened and lit up all the way to the control room and officiation chamber.

Like the previous officiation, the round glass chamber sprang to life, and the door slid open, inviting Jo.

On the wall monitor, messages flashed asking Ciaran to verify. He did, and the officiation process was kick-started. As soon as Jo stepped inside the glass chamber, the door shut and sealed. The glass spun. Magnificent blue and white light poured down on Jo in a cone shape.

All the energy channels were connected to the top of the glass chamber. Jo's body glowed.

Then as expected, before the process completed, a text message appeared on the screen. *"A source of energy has been corrupted and replaced by an alternative source. Please enter the ennead code to confirm your acceptance of the alternative source of energy."* Jo looked at Ciaran. Having had no time to do any research, Ciaran said, "Geb."

Jo nodded and entered the code.

Geb was the fourth god in the ennead. Given the first one worked for Madeline, the seventh one worked for Tadgh, he could only hope the forth worked for Jo.

On the monitor, a line of alarming red text appeared. *"Access denied."*

"What the fuck does that mean?" Tadgh shouted.

A harsh red light flashed all over Ciaran's control panel. Jo tried to type, but the control panel from inside the chamber denied her access altogether. Tadgh kicked the glass chamber door, trying to open it.

Ciaran tried several commands to adjust and reverse the codes. The machine spit out one rejection after another. Madeline stood behind him, her hand on his shoulder so he knew she was there.

Ayana circled the glass chamber like a leopard. She drew her Sciphil sword as if it could somehow help.

The glass chamber spun, shrieked, and spun again as if the chamber itself was looking for a solution.

Tears rolled down Jo's face when she saw Tadgh desperately trying to break the door. She mouthed to Tadgh, "I love you."

On Ciaran's control panel, a red line of text appeared. *"Too many failed attempts. Access denied."* The machine had kicked Ciaran out.

The glass chamber spun. The door swung open, and a force inside ejected Jo. She fell out, rolling on the floor. Tadgh darted over, grabbing her and pulling her into his arms.

The door of the glass chamber shut.

The entire tower shook. The energy inside the tower vibrated and whirled like an caged tornado.

"We're doomed. Eudaiz has ended," Ayana muttered.

Ciaran grabbed Madeline and pulled her into his arms.

The floor shook so hard that everyone was tumbling to the floor and sliding around like rag dolls.

Madeline and Ciaran clung to each other. Tadgh and Jo held each other. Ayana braced her hands on the control panel, watching the glass chamber and waiting for everything to explode.

CHAPTER 21

The Master strode into his secret bunker in Xiilok so quickly he startled Kyle. In a dark and stuffy room with no window, no fresh air, no life, Kyle scrambled up from a squeaky chair. "Mas—" The Master threw a sword at Kyle. It pierced his body and pinned him to the wall. A stream of blood trickled from Kyle's mouth.

"When you call me Master, you should know the word *means* something. Do you really think your pathetic ambush could kill me? Do you think you destroyed your own keystone and snatched the girl from Eudaiz so that Sciphil Four position couldn't be replaced, and Eudaiz would collapse?"

The Master pressed the sword harder. Kyle's eyes were glassy, and more blood trickled from his mouth. "I didn't kill you, Kyle. The LeBlancs didn't destroy you. You were killed by your own greed. If you can't have Eudaiz, you'd rather destroy it so no one can have it? You're stupid and greedy, Kyle."

Kyle's face was turning redder by the second. Then his entire body burst into flame and exploded. The Master covered his face to avoid shrapnel from the explosion. When he looked back, his sword was still pinned to the wall. From it hung a ragged piece of cloth that used to be Kyle's clothing.

Kyle himself had vanished.

***

In Tower Four, the energy vibration had subsided. The tower had stopped shaking, and the air had settled. Madeline was still in Ciaran's arms, and Jo was still in Tadgh's.

The tower had returned to its imposing quietness.

Ciaran's main control panel flashed. *"The ennead code has been deleted. All energy sources have been restored. Congratulations and Welcome, Sciphil Four, Josephine Cassidy."*

Jo stood up and glared at the machine.

"Bloody hell. Should we thank it?" Tadgh asked, a bit annoyed.

Ciaran approached and typed in a command to accept the adjustment. "Someone has a vested interest in Eudaiz. So much so that he installed the ennead code and then took it off when it was about to destroy Eudaiz. He wanted to create chaos, but he didn't want to destroy Eudaiz or kill its citizens. He's powerful and competent. He can place the code and take it off. Just like that." Ciaran looked at Ayana. "Do you have a theory about who that might be?"

Ayana shook her head. "During Bran's kingship, Kyle was the only internal problem. Our other enemies all came from the outside."

Ciaran shook his head. "The enemies back then appeared to be from the outside. But I don't believe this is an outside job."

"Can we sort this out tomorrow? It's been a long day." Tadgh wrapped his arm around Jo's shoulders and grinned.

***

In Sciphil Three residence, Ciaran sat at the side of the bed and reached his left wrist out so Madeline could apply the antidote patch. She looked at his God-given face and smiled. "I know you've tried, but you just don't look meek enough!" she said.

"Madeline, I—"

She locked her lips with his to stop him from talking. When she finished, she said, "Let me say it first. I'm sorry. I should have discussed my plans with you." She nudged him down to the bed so he lay on his back, and she climbed on top of him.

"I—"

"I haven't finished, Ciaran. I know you love me and our children, and I know there is no other woman between us . . . at the moment—"

"But—"

"Shhhh." She put a thumb on his lips. "But you did call me a snit. So as punishment, you have to lie here and take it . . ." Her hands started to roam over his body. His breath caught quickly. In this relationship, he wasn't the only one with clever hands.

"Go easy on me, First Councillor. I'm . . . injured." He gripped the mattress for purchase. His eyes rolled up with pleasure.

The robot walked into the room, and an orange light flashed on his face, whatever that meant. Madeline rolled her eyes and climbed off Ciaran.

"Isn't knocking a part of your programmed behavior?" Ciaran snarled at the robot as he sat up.

"I flashed the green light at the door twice. I can increase it to four times if you wish."

"That's not the same thing as knocking. When you knock, you can only enter the room after I answer. If I don't, then you don't enter the room. Understood?"

"Negative. Knocking on a door isn't a function available to me."

"I can certainly install it."

"Please ensure the functionality is compatible with other installed programs. Mine are complicated because I am a first generation robot."

"You know what? I'll change your name, too. Robert the robot just doesn't sound right."

"I agree," Madeline said.

"Affirmative. When would you like me to schedule the name change activity?" the robot asked.

Now it was Ciaran who rolled his eyes. "Okay, what are you here for?"

"A quick reminder of your upcoming schedule of important events. In two days, you need to replace Sciphil Five, Juliette LeBlanc."

"It's Juliette Dubois," Ciaran corrected.

"According to the records, her last name was—"

"I will fix your records. Now get out of here, Robert!" Ciaran snarled.

"Bran placed a note in the system that if you fail to kill Juliette and replace her in time, she will be invincible, and the consequence to Eudaiz will be catastrophic. Would you like me to print out his note?"

"No. If you want to protect your motherboard, you'd better get out of this room right now, Robert."

The robot shot down the little wheels on his feet and scurried out.

"He actually muttered some profanity. Did you hear that?" Ciaran asked Madeline.

Madeline smiled and climbed onto Ciaran's lap. "It's not Robert who's bothering you. It's Juliette who ticked you off. She's your past. There's nothing we can do about it. We'll deal with her tomorrow." And then she pushed him gently down to the bed again.

PART TWO

DOUBLED BISHOPS

CHAPTER 22

The melting ice on top of the mountain was slippery. One misstep, and he could land at the bottom of the canyon, awaiting his death. But he kept advancing against the blizzard despite an inner voice screaming inside his head, "Turn back, Bran! It's not your fight!"

But he knew in his conscience, it *was* his fight. Bran LeBlanc, king of Eudaiz, the universe that promised its citizens safety and happiness. What kind of a king would he be if he left a newborn alone in this dangerous situation?

He wasn't foolish. He knew the Daimon Gate wasn't his territory. Neither was it his jurisdiction. The huge canyon in front of him might be merely an illusion. The bone-chilling cold and the haunting howls emanating from space creatures somewhere could easily defeat weak souls.

But not him.

He would never give in to a group of soulless and heartless space creatures who wanted nothing more than to terrorize his universe.

He had to find and save the child at any cost.

"Stop!" he yelled at a shadow running past him. He needn't look nor ask—he knew it was Kyle Wolf, the traitor of Eudaiz.

Kyle was Sciphil Four, one of those Sciphils that had several talents and so much potential. Bran had seen the potential and had gone against the advice other councillors had given to appoint Kyle.

The shadow didn't stop, so Bran gave chase. In no time, he had forced Kyle up against the slippery edge of the canyon.

"Leave the baby, and I'll let you live. Go away. Never come back to Eudaiz again, Kyle," Bran said, gauging the basket Kyle was carrying.

"You don't have to the play head games with me, Bran. I'm young, but I know forgiving isn't part of your human DNA," Kyle snarled.

"You're right, I'm not forgiving you that easily. But let's not put an innocent child between us."

"Innocent?" Kyle laughed bitterly. "Maybe now . . ."

"Madeline is innocent. How is taking Chiara's child going to earn you her love, Kyle?" Bran asked and slowly approached Kyle. Behind Kyle was the sharp edge of a cliff.

"Love?" Kyle laughed harder and waved the basket in front of him. "You think this is about love? I'll never have Chiara. I know that for a fact. I've come to terms with that."

"So why did you take the baby?"

Kyle's laughter faded, and his eyes sparked with rage and insanity. "She's not just any baby. Madeline will one day become a female Sciphil..." He lowered his voice to a growl, "What I don't have, no one can have . . ."

"A Eudaizian can never have the kingship—"

"No . . . no, you're mistaken. Kingship is given. Silver Blood is what I want. It's what you want as well, isn't it?" Kyle said.

"Silver Blood is a myth!" Bran snarled.

"Really? So you're mentoring Ayana out of the goodness of your heart? Is that what you're saying? She's your protégé, and you're not building her up to take the first fall for your Silver Blood?" Kyle smirked. He approached Bran. "That foolish girl is going to do anything for you. You think you're brilliant, but you know nothing, Bran. There are people much more powerful than you. Much worse. They want Silver Blood more badly than you. They want Eudaiz more than you. And they'll get it."

Bran drew his sword, pointing it at Kyle's chest. "I don't take Eudaiz for granted."

Kyle reached out the hand in which he held the basket with the baby inside, dangling it over the cliff. "You wouldn't want to hurt me, Bran. My hand might slip. Let me go. I never said you take Eudaiz for granted. I know you've worked hard for it. So hard that you will need Silver Blood to protect it. You'll fight for it at any cost."

"Ayana is a rightful Sciphil. You say one more word to smear her reputation, and I'll pierce this sword through your heart. *That* is what I will do at any cost."

Kyle laughed and took a step forward. Bran said nothing further and swung his sword at Kyle. Kyle jerked back to avoid the deadly blade. The smile had vanished from his face. He pivoted quickly and kicked the snow so that the ice blasted at Bran. Bran staggered back. Seizing the opportunity, Kyle fled.

Bran couldn't let Kyle go free. He disliked attacking a man from behind, but Kyle had given him no choice. He thrust the sword forward toward Kyle's back, but Kyle suddenly turned back toward him, placing the baby basket right in the path of the sword.

Bran withdrew immediately. He shuddered. It had almost been too late. Before he could wield another attack on Kyle, he felt the impact of Kyle's foot on his abdomen. His body flew over the edge of the slippery cliff. He dropped his sword and used both hands to grab a small piece of frozen rock protruding several feet down.

He dangled, hanging onto the piece of ice with his bare fingers. From the top of the cliff, Kyle looked down at him. "The Silver Blood is more real than ever. Now that you will die soon, I might as well return to Eudaiz and claim the kingship and the Silver Blood. Thanks for the opportunity, Bran."

Kyle stomped on the edge of the cliff. The ice cracked, broke, and fell to the base of the canyon. Along with Bran.

CHAPTER 23

Madeline stared at the white ceiling for a long time but couldn't seem to drift back to sleep. The dome-shaped ceiling was almost transparent. It was made of an incredibly strong material. Ciaran had once explained the purpose of the specially designed ceiling to her, but she couldn't remember what he'd said except that it had something to do with energy. She didn't care much for technology.

In the dark, something was bothering her. Something was wrong.

It was the first time they'd had genuine tranquility since they had been in Eudaiz. Their children were safe with their grandparents in the Daimon Gate. The system had informed them about the urgency of replacing Sciphil Five, and Ciaran had made arrangements for the recruitment of a Sciphil Five replacement.

The dilemma of Sciphil Five came as no surprise to them. Juliette was Ciaran's ex-wife. She'd disappeared from Earth several years ago. Everyone—including his mother—had been telling Ciaran all along that Juliette had married him for the LeBlancs' fortune and privileges.

But it didn't matter whether he believed what they told him or not, Ciaran was a man of his own strong will. He loved Juliette, and he knew she loved him. The most painful truth was that, unbeknownst to him, Juliette's father was Sciphil Five, and he had always planned to place her into the LeBlancs to obtain their secrets.

Ciaran was the last one to know about what the others called Juliette's betrayal. She came back to Earth as Sciphil Five, and she wanted to kill Ciaran.

To protect himself, his family, and Madeline, Ciaran had killed Juliette on Earth. That was what he thought.

He didn't realize his actions on Earth had pushed Juliette back into her tower in Eudaiz where no one but the king had access. Safe in her tower, if Juliette reformed, she would become invincible. Therefore, immediate termination was necessary, and her replacement had to be ready.

But deep down, Madeline knew her husband still believed there had been love between them. If he didn't, he wouldn't be the husband she had fallen in love with.

In the dark, Madeline turned toward Ciaran and found his back facing her. That was rare. Even in his sleep, he always leaned toward her. At times, he lay on his back, but he wouldn't face away from her.

Unable to see his face, she wrapped her arm around his shoulder and inched closer to him. Their bodies fit to each other, just like pieces of a jigsaw puzzle that were meant to be together. Feeling her embrace, he stirred and turned toward her.

Then she saw his eyes. In the dark, his striking gray eyes were staring right at her.

"Hey, sorry I woke you . . ." She touched his face when her psychic mind told her that something in his eyes wasn't entirely him. Something unusual was going on in his mind.

He didn't respond to her, just gazed at her face in the dark.

"Ciaran!"

Suddenly, his hands were all over her. He reached over and kissed her. But the usual heat of passion and love wasn't there. This was primal. His hands on her body was a demand for sex. His kisses on her lips and everywhere else oozed with the inexplicable feel of mysterious power.

His mouth ravished hers. He was on top of her, and he took her as if there would be no tomorrow. He pushed and plunged into her as if his life depended on it. His usual finesse was gone. The tempting, urging, and loving was missing. His irresistible lovemaking skills were absent. He just took and took.

It wasn't her husband who was making love to her.

Ciaran could be rough and tough, but he was never selfish when they were intimate.

"No, Ciaran, you're hurting me," she said. She wasn't really hurt. But with Ciaran, she didn't even need to say no before he stopped. That was the kind of man he was. That was the husband she knew. So she demanded him to stop.

It didn't surprise her when he—or the thing that had taken him over—didn't listen.

He was overwhelmingly strong. His full body weight was on her. He pushed and shoved. He demanded. She couldn't get out from under him.

"Ciaran, stop!"

He kept pushing. She pulled at the sheet and tried to get away without success. She pulled so hard she tore the sheet off. He rolled her over so she was on top. Taking the opportunity, she hopped off. He pulled her back from behind and pinned her down again. She kicked the light on the bedside table. The light and everything else on the table crashed to the floor. She pushed him over and jumped off the bed, running toward the bathroom. He caught her again. She grabbed at a chair for purchase. He snatched the chair and threw it to the wall. It fell into pieces.

In a short moment, after crashing several pieces of future in the room, he hauled her back to the bed and pinned her down. He continued to satisfy his sexual demand until he climaxed violently and collapsed next to her in a heap of sweat.

She lay still for a long moment, trying to digest what had just happened. After a while, Ciaran stirred and opened his eyes. Then, she saw his true look, the intensity in his eyes, the love and care of the husband she knew so well. He looked at her and frowned. He sat up abruptly, surveying the torn sheet and the condition of the room.

He scrambled out of the bed. "I . . . what did I do?" he asked. The look on his face was more devastating than any answer she could give him to describe what he, or the thing inside him, had just done.

She considered her response carefully before giving it to him. "You were a bit more enthusiastic than usual during our intimate activities." She smiled.

His eyes darkened. He looked down at his body, looked at her, and then glanced around the room. She knew she didn't have a poker face. But she thought she could at least manufacture a neutral expression until they figured out how to handle this.

She knew it hadn't been him.

Ciaran paced back and forth in the room. His eyes were so intense that if they could shoot bullets, the walls would have turned into a cratered moonscape. He came to the bed and crouched at the bedside. He brushed aside the hair that dangled on her forehead.

"Did I hurt you? Tell me the truth."

She sat up and looked into his eyes. "It wasn't physical pain . . ."

He pulled the sleeve of her nightgown up and saw the bruises that had started to form. She pulled the sleeve back down. She could feel his hand shake when he brushed away the hair on her shoulder and saw the bruises.

He stood up and stepped back, looking pale as a ghost. "I . . . I raped you . . ."

She stood up and approached him. "No, Ciaran. I know what rape is. You were forceful. But you didn't rape me. I said no because I want . . ."

"You said no?" He gestured widely. "You said no, and I continued to do this?"

"It wasn't you," she stated as firmly as possible and advanced. He stepped back. "Don't back away from me, Ciaran, because that hurts me more than anything."

He stared at her for a moment. There was nothing on his face but devastation and confusion. "I need some time by myself," he said and strode out of the room.

CHAPTER 24

An inviting eighteen-color rainbow arched over a green field. It looked like an invitation to him, but maybe it was in appearance only. Zach Flynn was an Australian musician, recruited to be a successor of Sciphil Two, Ayana Dee, only a short time ago. He went through the Daimon Gate at the same time as Ciaran, Madeline, and Tadgh. As far as that experience went, the trip and the Sciphil tests were enough to scar him for life. He had all the reasons in the multiverse to dislike the Daimon Gate.

Nothing here appeared as it should be. Nothing was real.

Ciaran had to recruit Dan from Earth to replace Sciphil Five. Dan was Sciphil Nine, Pete Chandler's, nephew and Zach's best friend. Ciaran thought Zach was in the best position to quickly convince Dan to join this elusive world of the multiverse. Regardless of the spins Ayana had put into the training at Sciphil Two residence, Zach was bored with it. He missed his music, his friends, and his family on Earth. So he had jumped at the chance to come back.

Ayana headed in the direction of the rainbow. "When you travel from Eudaiz to Earth via the Daimon Gate, the rainbows usually mark the exit zones at both ends," she said.

"Well, when we exited to Eudaiz for the first time, it looked like a gothic dome!" Zach frowned in confusion.

"When you see a gothic dome, that means either you or your companion is doing something wrong to cheat the system in the Daimon Gate, and the gate was about to kill the sinner." Ayana looked off to the distance. A flash of sorrow crossed her magnificent blue eyes.

Ayana appeared to be in her fifties. To Zach, she looked like an angel. Her hair was as white as cloud, cascading down her body like pieces of silk. Her angelic face always smiled at him. Her striking blue eyes were seas of mysteries. Zach didn't know her true Eudaizian age. Hell, he didn't even know his own Eudaizian age. He was thirty-one on Earth. But he must be a kid in Eudaiz. Or teenager. Ayana was going out of her way to try to spice up his training so he wasn't bored. But he was. He was bored out of his skull! *Shit*. He had to stop behaving like a teen here.

The piece of land in front of them suddenly moved aside, stood up, and cracked open like the mouth of a cave. Zach pulled Ayana toward his back. They both staggered backward a few steps.

"I'm your Sciphil, Zach. I'll protect you, not the other way around," Ayana said.

Zach smiled. "That's an ingrained habit from Earth. I'm still a man, you see. And because of that, my human standards apply. I won't let a woman face danger to protect me."

"That's gender discrimination, isn't it? Plus, that moving cave is just a dimensional shift. It happens all the time in the Daimon Gate. It's not dangerous by any means."

"Well, Ayana, these same activities almost swallowed us alive when we went through last time."

"You were in the middle of your Sciphil tests, Zach. Now that you've qualified as a Sciphil successor, there won't be a problem with dimensional shift unless you attempt to do something wrong—"

A small crack suddenly appeared on the cave wall, looking similar to a firing hole in a tower. Zach pushed Ayana back and wielded a blade of sound in his mind. He sent it straight toward the hole in the wall.

Zach had the ability to think of sound as tangible object, bend it into any shape he wanted, and then send it into people's minds. He had done that on Earth since he was a kid, mostly to annoy people. Apparently, in Eudaiz, they called it sound-bending, and that annoying little skill was considered a talent here. That was why Ayana had recruited him.

"Get back!" Zach shouted and pulled at Ayana, who had unsheathed her sword to fight. Zach sent another wave of sharp sound at the wall, making it crack further. It slid open, turning into an eye and a mouth.

A voice emanated from the mouth. "*Ayana is a rightful Sciphil. You say one more word that smears her reputation, and I will pierce this sword through your heart. That is what I will do at all costs.*"

"That was Bran's voice," Ayana whispered and approached the wall. A large area of it had shaped itself into something like the wizened face of an old man. "You're the stone observer . . ." she said and reached her hand out to touch the face emerging in the wall.

"Hey, don't touch him!" Zach pulled her back.

"He's the stone observer, Zach. He's harmless."

Zach rolled his eyes.

"Eye rolling shows disrespect to the elderly," said the stone observer.

"No shit," Zach muttered.

"No shit," the stone observer mocked Zach's Australian accent.

"You saw Bran? What did he say about me? Who did he talk to?" Ayana asked.

"I couldn't see him. Ice covered my eyes. He woke me at the cliff with his loud fight, and then he hung onto what used to be my nose on the way down into the oblivion hole. I captured the conversation he had with the person who pushed him into that hole."

Tears welled in Ayana's eyes. "Do you mind replaying it for me?"

The stone observer sighed. The conversation between Bran and Kyle before Kyle kicked Bran down the canyon was played back in their voices via the stone observer's mouth.

"Thirty-three years ago, he still sounded the same. It felt just like yesterday. Silver Blood. Bran believed in the Silver Blood!" Ayana whispered as tears rolled down her face.

"He said it's a myth, Ayana," Zach said.

She shook her head. "If he thought it was a myth, he would have told me. He didn't say anything to me because he believes it exists—"

"And he didn't want you to do it." Zach asked, his voice still a bit shaky. He had a gut feeling that Ayana was soon going to try to do something unthinkable. He didn't need Madeline's psychic ability or Ciaran's laser sharp brain to know

Ayana loved Bran—the mountain-moving, ocean-crossing kind of love.

Whatever the story between her and Bran was, whatever the Silver Blood was, this information was no good to her. Zach made a mental note to discuss it with Ciaran at length when he came back. It was obvious that Bran had disappeared thirty-three years before Ciaran found him in the oblivion hole when he went through the Daimon Gate for the first time. Zach shuddered as he recalled the incident.

Bran was a prominent figure. In his thirty-three years in the hole, he had still been in charge of Eudaiz and had still plotted and planned many things in Eudaiz and on Earth. The moment he came back, he had been killed. Zach shook his head, thinking about how uncertain life could be. "All right. I'll go back to Earth to get Dan. We'll fix the Sciphil Five problem and then move on to Silver Blood."

"It's not your problem, Zach."

"But it's yours, so it's now mine. I'm your successor. Can you promise me you won't do anything drastic before I come back?"

"All right." Ayana pointed in the direction of the rainbow. "Let's go," she said and led the way. Zach turned toward the stone observer. "Old man, I don't think you mean any harm, but why did you tell her what you did? Bran and Kyle are both dead now. That information only devastates her."

"It's not my call."

"It's your memory and your mouth, both of which you have total control of by the way!"

"I'm a stone observer. I listen, and I tell stories. She was a topic of interest in that conversation. She asked, and I had to tell her."

"What's Silver Blood?"

The stone observer sighed. "That's not my story to tell."

Zach shook his head and turned around to follow Ayana.

"Young man."

"What?" Zach snarled.

"Come back later. I'll tell you a story in which you are the topic of interest."

"My problem might be of interest to someone or something in the multiverse, but let me tell you this—I am not interested in your story. I made a promise to Ayana, and I intend fulfill it. I have a duty to Eudaiz, which I will live up to. Whatever happens in this Daimon Gate, I couldn't care less. So keep the story to yourself."

The stone observer sighed again. Zach mumbled some profanity and turned to leave. Then he heard the stone observer mutter, "You're a good Sciphil Two. But Ayana is good, too. What a shame!"

"What are you saying? What will happen to Ayana? And what does that have to do with me?" Zach turned around and snarled through his teeth. But the stone observer had fallen back into his deep sleep and no longer responded.

"Zach? We're running late." Ayana called from a distance. Zach glared at the sleeping stone man one more time and turned on his heel.

CHAPTER 25

Madeline pushed at the double door at the end of the hallway to enter the control area of Sciphil Three residence. Ciaran hadn't come back to the bed chamber. There was no way she would let him hide out in the control room and use the universe's matter as his shield. They had to talk this out. It wasn't like him at all to avoid a problem.

The security light above the double steel door glared down at her, blinking and scanning. She was sure that was a robotic eye-rolling gesture. If it could feel any pain at all, she would have given it a knuckle punch right now.

She tried to psychically peek into Ciaran's mind several times without success. He knew her too well. Most importantly, he now knew how to block her out of his head. She couldn't forget the look in his eyes when something had taken him over—and the look of those same beautiful eyes when he came back to her. Confusion. The fact that she'd lied to him about what had happened didn't help. But she still thought they could always figure things out together.

The door didn't budge. She stepped back and saw the control panel on the wall. She placed her right palm on it to verify.

"Good morning, Madeline LeBlanc, Sciphil One," a robotic voice said.

"You are one hundred percent right, machine. I'm Sciphil One. Now open the door!" Nothing happened. "Please!" she added.

"Your access to this area has been denied."

She put her hands on her hips. "Excuse me?"

"What would you like me to excuse you for?" the computer spat out.

"I need to talk to Ciaran."

"Your access to this area has been denied," the computer repeated in its monotone voice.

She waved her arms in the air, realizing there was no point arguing with a computer. She turned around and saw Robert, the home robot, approaching. "Good morning—"

"Ciaran didn't respond to his wrist unit," she interrupted. "I need to know what's going on. Let me in," she snarled, pointing at the door.

"I can't alter Ciaran's programs," Robert said.

"Ciaran *programmed* it to lock me out? Is that what you're saying?"

"Based on my calculation, there is a high probability that my answer would trigger negative emotions in you, Madeline. I can't give you access, but I can give you this information. Ciaran isn't in the control room. He left for the council meeting."

"There isn't a council meeting this morning!" she exclaimed.

"Yes, there is. It's an urgent meeting regarding Sciphil Five replacement."

Madeline narrowed her eyes. "I didn't see any invitation. I'm the first councillor, and I don't recall resigning!" She turned around and strode angrily away. Robert spun the little wheels on his feet and scurried after her.

"Madeline, I have a piece of data that I think I should reveal to you."

"I'd think Ciaran would have programmed you to not talk to me as well! Aren't you supposed to know what information I do and don't have access to?" Madeline snarled again. She wasn't sure if Robert could read her tone or merely understand what she said. His robotic eyes blinked rapidly, and he appeared to be processing an enormous amount of information. She swore she saw smoke coming out of his ears. "I've got to go to the meeting that I am uninvited to, Robert."

"There is a ninety percent chance that the information I am going to give you is relevant to your interests. This is provided by an alternate program that Bran had given me. I can learn from human emotions. Ciaran didn't know about this, and thus he didn't block your access to this piece of information."

Madeline arched an eyebrow. "Now you've got me interested. What do you have for me?"

"Ciaran blocked my access to the data of what happened in your bed chamber, so this analysis isn't based on that."

"Let's keep it that way." Madeline rolled her eyes. "Tell me the part that isn't related to our bedroom activities, please."

"I started my usual scan on Ciaran this morning before he could stop me. This partial scan revealed that there is a small amount of unusual energy running inside Ciaran. It is non-Eudaizian energy, and it's not natural. I couldn't tell Ciaran because the analysis was done using the program Ciaran didn't have access to."

"If he didn't have access to it, why are you telling me?"

"Bran designed this program to protect Ciaran. When his mind is acting against him, Ciaran doesn't have access, but a person who has his best interests in mind *would* have access. That person is you—his spouse."

"Is that energy going to kill him or harm him in any way?"

"That's inconclusive. If he meets the demand of the energy source, it will make him stronger. If not, it will explode his central nervous system. It arouses his sexual urges and requires a significant amount of sexual activity to match the demand of the energy source. Ciaran's psychological profile indicates that he prefers female sexual counterparts, so I think—"

"That's enough, Robert. So you're saying there's a source of artificial energy inside Ciaran that makes him strong, but he has to have sex like a rabbit to meet its demand. Is that all, or is there something else he has to do to stay alive?"

"I don't have any information about the sexual activities a rabbit needs. That is an Earth animal I don't have data on. Nor do I have access to run experiments in order to collect data. However, Ciaran's mental capacity is extremely strong, and he has the ability to resist the urge to engage in sexual activities with women other than you."

Madeline nodded. "And he doesn't know doing that is going to kill him."

"Affirmative. He seemed to have had enough energy to run for today. But I am unsure about tomorrow. Given that it is a new source of energy,

I am unsure whether we can drain it off. I don't have enough data to draw conclusions on whether it's a medical or metaphysical problem."

"By any chance, do you know how the energy got into him?" Madeline asked.

"I located the entry point. It wasn't airborne and wasn't digested or injected. It came from a medical patch and penetrated via his left wrist."

Madeline fell numb. Robert said something else, but she was no longer listening. Her head started ringing. She knew why the strange energy was inside him.

She had put it there.

CHAPTER 26

Ciaran strode out of the council meeting which he had dismissed early. They hadn't given him what he expected. The pipe-shaped corridor was empty, but it didn't mean no activities were going on. This was a restricted area, and thus, no creatures without authority and relevant passes could enter. Behind each white column in the corridor were security cameras controlled by central robots. He could flip open any wall panel and gain access to the control patch that would recognize his palm print. He could make the system do whatever he wanted.

The light came through the semitransparent ceiling, casting a sheen of dim white onto the floor. It wasn't natural light but a source of purest energy that had been absorbed from the cosmos, purified through multiple layers and pumped into the air of the Sciphil zone. They had the best of the best where energy was concerned. And that was why Eudaiz was the most attractive target in the cosmos.

Ciaran looked at his hands. They were still a bit shaky after the experience with Madeline in the bed chamber. He glanced up and down the corridor, trying to make sense of the energy processes. He had a duty to protect Eudaiz's energy. Billions of lives depended on it. But who would protect him from what was inside him right now?

As soon as he left the bed chamber, he had run tests on himself and had detected a foreign source of energy. It wasn't possible for him to pinpoint its point of origin. He'd been to Xiilok, the land of the multiversal outlaws, and to Black Rock. He'd been in and out of dimensional holes and pipes countless times. Anything could have gotten into him at any point.

The double steel door slid open, and his brother, Tadgh, strode out. "What the heck was that about?" Tadgh asked.

"You're Sciphil Seven, and that was your first official meeting. What's the problem?"

"I'd be the biggest dumbass in the cosmos if I believed you. Sciphil One, Madeline, Sciphil Two, Ayana, Sciphil Four, Jo and Sciphil Six, Janie were not at that meeting. Unless you're conducting a separate meeting with the female councillors, maybe we need a unisex meeting room next time?"

"All right, it wasn't an official meeting. I just needed some information from the male councillors. But not from you, of course—you don't have the experience."

"Well, apparently those walking-talking trees of knowledge didn't give you what you needed. And I don't think I have the answers for you. But why did you keep asking them about energy that draws from gender-specific sources? Are you planning some genetic engineering projects? Wait, you've already done that! What's the news?"

"I don't know."

"Bullshit. You always know."

Ciaran glances at his still shaking hands. He balled them into fists and shoved them into his pockets. "We have to deal with the Sciphil Five officiation, Tadgh. It won't be easy. I need you to concentrate on the bigger picture here."

"Give me an example of anything easy or unimportant that we've had to deal with since setting foot in this universe, Ciaran. I can't think of any. You might not think your personal issue is important, but brother, you're as white as a sheet. And what's with the shaky hands? If anything happens to you, I have no idea what shit to do. Let alone worrying about saving your universe . . ."

Ciaran looked up at the semitransparent ceilings again, contemplating the way the energy filtered down into the hallway. Then he looked at his brother. "I was rather more enthusiastic than usual during our intimacy last night."

Tadgh grinned. "No information is too much information when it comes to sex."

"You asked."

"Go on!"

"Well, that was Madeline's polite version of the situation. My version is—I raped her.

201

Something took me over, and I forced myself on her. You should see the bruises on her body."

"You're mistaken, Ciaran. I don't know jack about human psychological profiles the way you do. But you've forgotten I have the unfortunate gift of feeling the emotions of Kyle's rape victims. You know how many times I've gotten into the heads of those girls when they were raped. And let me tell you, regardless how strong you think you are, you're not capable of causing that kind of damage. Don't flatter yourself."

Ciaran stared at his brother. He was being narrow-minded and didn't see the big picture. It didn't matter what *he* thought he did. It was what Madeline said he did to her that mattered. She understood him. And he didn't understand himself. *Stupid!* he scolded himself. "You're right, Tadgh . . ." Suddenly, a female voice whispered into his ears.

"Go to Gaia, Ciaran."

The voice had a strange accent. It sang like bells. Every word vibrated against his nervous system and felt as if it was tearing it into pieces. *Control!* Ciaran told himself. That was what he was best at—controlling his mind and his body.

Energy leaked from every pore in his body, rolling off of him in waves. Blood trickled from his nose. He grunted, his knees buckled, and he slumped to the floor. He felt Tadgh grabbing his shoulders but couldn't hear what he was saying.

"Who's that?" he asked and prepared himself for another wave of pain from the voice.

"What's inside you is a harmful source of foreign energy. You have to get it out. Go to Gaia."

"Gaia is just a kid. You can see what's it's doing to me. I can't let it get inside Gaia."

"She's a conduit. She was made to transfer energy. She'll be fine."

"Wh-who are you?" He didn't really care much to hear the answer. He was on the verge of passing out. *Control! Keep it together!* he told himself.

Then the voice vanished. The pressure in the air lifted. Tadgh's voice and face became clear again.

"Who the fuck were you talking to? Can you get up?" Tadgh asked but helped Ciaran up without waiting for an answer.

Ciaran stood, leaning against the wall. "I need to go to Gaia. She and her father are staying in the guest wing in Sciphil Three residence."

Tadgh nodded. "You can barely walk. Come on, let's go." Tadgh wrapped Ciaran's arm around his shoulders, and they made their way to the side door to get to a capsule platform. In the capsule, Ciaran verified and entered the command. They departed smoothly.

The impact was incredible. It was as if they had been hit by a missile. The capsule stopped, dangling dead on its rail. Ciaran punched the door open. "Jump!" he shouted and jumped out of the capsule. Tadgh followed just before the wires in the capsule sparked with fire, and an explosion tore through the capsule.

The rail was quite close to the ground. In fact, the jump was only about ten feet. Ciaran was dizzy. The air was too thin. He didn't recognize where they were. They must still be in the Sciphil central zone. It was supposed to be safe.

"Are you okay, Tadgh?"

"Yep . . ." Tadgh stood up, wiped his face, and coughed out some dirt.

Dirt? Ciaran frowned. There was no dirt in the Sciphil central zone. This looked more like a desert. He could barely stand. What if they had to fight? In front of them, five space creatures emerged from the sand. And not just any creatures—Ciaran knew they were Xiiloks, the worst kind of multiversal outlaws that killed for money.

"Right, five hulks against one human. How's that for a fair fight?" Tadgh asked sarcastically.

Ciaran glared at him.

"Well, one and half against five. Still unfair," Tadgh mumbled.

A wave of fireballs flew at them from the guns of the five creatures. And the bodies of Tadgh and Ciaran flew into the air like rag dolls.

CHAPTER 27

Agitated, Madeline paced back and forth in the capsule. Robert, their home robot, was manning the control panel. The interactive map on the monitor showed their progress to Sciphil Six residence. They would be there in no time. But it felt as if it had taken forever. She needed to use the gateway via Sciphil Six residence to go to iilos again to see Moira, Ciaran's five-hundred-year-old ancestor.

Madeline smiled on the inside when she recalled Robert's confusion when she explained to him that the i in iilos shouldn't be capitalized.

Moira didn't give Madeline an explanation for the strange name, but she wagered that Moira had a sentimental reason for doing so. Because the robot wouldn't understand the sentiment, she simply gave the instructions.

Due to a disagreement between Ciaran and Moira, she had poisoned him. Madeline had talked her out of her short-sighted rage and had gained the antidote for Ciaran. He didn't want it and thought he could figure out a cure himself. But she had forced it on him. Now she knew it was that medical patch that had put the strange energy into Ciaran.

She didn't think Moira wanted to kill Ciaran. But even if the side effect of the antidote wasn't intentional, she needed to know what it was and how to remove it. She'd told Robert that, and in his unique way of problem solving, he suggested going to Moira for a sample of the antidote. He could analyze it and figure out the next step.

It turned out to be quite convenient because Robert was able to help her drive this stupid vehicle called a capsule. She promised herself that after they had gotten through this ordeal and she had some time for herself, she'd go to a driving school—if they had such a thing in Eudaiz.

Moira's residence was the same as it had been before—a weird Irish country house in the middle of an artificial Irish countryside. Madeline stormed into the grand hall without an invitation and found Moira stood next to the fireplace, waiting.

"My system alerted me that you might be coming without warning. What can I do for you?" Moira smiled graciously and then arched an eyebrow at Robert. "This must be Bran's home robot!"

"Yes, I am the first generation of—"

"The antidote you gave Ciaran has side effects," Madeline interrupted.

"What kind of side effects?"

"Based on Robert's analysis, the energy creates strong urges for sexual activity . . ."

"That's the robotic analysis. What's your view, Madeline? You journalists always have one. Plus you share a bedroom with him, don't you?"

Madeline approached, looking at Moira in the eye. The woman had a pretentious smile pasted on her face, but in her eyes, Madeline saw genuine concern.

"It felt as though something had taken him over. He had sex as if his life depended on it. And then he didn't recall anything afterward."

"It won't be fatal, I suppose."

"I can't draw that conclusion until I get a sample of your antidote you gave me for your poison," Robert said.

"I beg your pardon?" Moira asked the robot. "Do you think I intentionally put that foreign energy into Ciaran? It's not supposed to be there. It's a formula for energy controllability."

"In theory, you can't control your energy. You either have it, or you don't," Robert quipped.

"In theory? Robot, you said so yourself. I don't do theory. It's *practice*," Moira growled.

"And your practice has proven to be defective. Tell me how to get rid of it!" Madeline demanded.

"Not possible."

"What do you mean, not possible. You had a way to put it in. You have to have a way to take it out!" Madeline exclaimed.

"It's a simulation of Silver Blood. I don't know how to take it out. I thought it was a myth!"

"You simulated a myth! What kind of insanity is that?" Madeline whirled around.

"It's supposed to be good for him. Silver Blood is the most powerful and controllable source of energy. It can heal the body of all injuries. It makes a person invincible. It can be distributed, stored, or turned on and off. It's the ultimate power in the cosmos. But it does draw initial energy from female sources."

"So tell me how to turn it off!" Madeline snarled.

"What's in Ciaran is my attempt at the Silver Blood. But it's not the actual thing! I don't know how to turn it off."

A sharp pain stabbed at Madeline's head—her psychic vision had caught her off guard. She grunted and grabbed at her head. In her mind, she saw Ciaran and Tadgh standing in a sandy area, injured and undefended in front of five enormous creatures. She breathed heavily. She felt dizzy. She had to do something. She had to help him.

"Ciaran and Tadgh are in trouble. Can you get my wrist unit to communicate with him, Robert?"

"I'm afraid not, Madeline. He blocked it this morning. I can't crack his codes."

She had to do something. She didn't know where he was. She turned toward Moira. "Your simulation of the Silver Blood, does it have power?"

"In theory, yes," Moira said.

CHAPTER 28

"Tadgh!" Ciaran called out. The desert-like sand wasn't kind to Ciaran's eyes. His vision was bloody, most likely from the impact of the explosion. He searched around for Tadgh. A few feet from him, his brother sat up. His arms and shoulders were bleeding. Ciaran darted over. "Are you okay?" he asked.

"Look at yourself before you ask me how I am, Ciaran."

Ciaran suddenly felt the pain in his arms, head, and back. He wiped his forehead and saw blood smears on his hand.

"Son of bitches. Do they really need those kinds of guns when there are five of them?" Tadgh scolded and pulled out his guns. The five hulks approached slowly.

Ciaran knew when he had an advantage. And when he didn't.

He could kill with his thoughts. That had always been his talent. If he wanted to, he could wield a blade of fury in his mind and chop these creatures into a hundred thousand pieces. But he needed strength to do so—a resource he didn't have much of at the moment. If he did it now, it would be like throwing tiny darts at those gigantic boards closing in on them.

"Run, Tadgh. We can't beat them."

"Run, my ass."

The creatures continued to advance, raising their guns again. He had to do something. Ciaran concentrated. He didn't bother pulling his guns out because he knew they would be a joke for those creatures. Their footsteps made the ground grumble. Then through the howling wind, the flying sand, and the roaring of the monsters, Ciaran heard a familiar voice—Madeline. She had channeled into his mind.

"Ciaran, use the foreign energy in you. It can ignite your blade of fury."

There was no other option and no time to think of anything else. Ciaran did what Madeline told him. He concentrated and gathered the energy source he had been avoiding all day. It surged up inside him like electric current. He could feel the tangibility of it—the strength it was giving him.

"Get down, Tadgh!" Ciaran shouted. Without a word, Tadgh dropped flat on the ground. Ciaran crouched, braced his hands on the ground, and did what he had done many times before. He concentrated, looked at the approaching creatures, and summoned the fury in his mind.

Like a tornado, it came—a spinning blade of death. In a short moment, the five creatures were transformed into pieces of substance, whatever it was. The material pooled but was quickly absorbed into the sand. He didn't see the familiar pool of swimming worms, but he was sure they were Xiilok creatures. As for who sent them, he had no clue. He wagered it might be Kyle because the robot had reported that the probability that Kyle was dead was negligible.

Kyle had always wanted to kill him. He needed only to interfere with the control system in Eudaiz, and the robot would send Ciaran's capsule to a place Ciaran hadn't intended to go.

The power of the foreign energy still lingered in him. Ciaran could feel the adrenaline. The gash on his back must be healing because the pain was fading by the second. The cuts on his arms were disappearing in front of his eyes. Judging by the look on Tadgh's face, it was the same with the wound on his forehead.

"Wow! That's cool. Whatever it is you have, I want some of it!" Tadgh said.

Ciaran chuckled. "It comes from the foreign energy inside me. You sure you want it?"

"Oh . . . in that case, no. I don't want it. No offense. Sex is quite good when performed voluntarily by both parties."

"Tadgh! I can't believe you said that."

"Sorry!"

Ciaran opened the control panel of his wrist unit and entered a command. Soon a rail-free capsule hovered above and landed next to them.

CHAPTER 29

Arriving at his Sciphil Three residence, Ciaran checked the security outside. Everything looked normal. He entered the residence and heard Gaia's faint laughter coming from the guest wing. He quickly turned in that direction. A housekeeper robot there zoomed over to greet Ciaran and ask if he needed anything. He dismissed the machine and continued on to the hall.

"Something spooky is going on here!" Tadgh whispered.

"I'll check it out—don't make a move when we're unsure."

"Roger that."

In the living room of the guest wing, Ciaran and Tadgh found Liam and Gaia. Ciaran contemplated. Gaia would have been the first Eudaizian citizen he and Madeline had met when they came to Eudaiz. The capsule had been attacked, and they landed just outside District Seven. Gaia had found them when he was out of it and Madeline was guarding him.

Since then, she had saved Ciaran several times using her ability to transfer energy. Ciaran tried to recall the moment they landed at the gate and the decision they had made. It seemed totally logical, and the meeting with Gaia could be purely coincidental.

Ciaran didn't believe in coincidences. But he hadn't yet come up with evidence to the contrary.

Liam's face showed a hint of something that Ciaran couldn't read just yet. He was finishing some kind of lesson with Gaia, but he stood to greet Ciaran. Gaia continued to laugh until tears streamed down her face. Ciaran glanced at the books on the table and looked at Liam.

"Don't you think it's a bit early to teach her this?" Ciaran asked, pointing to the pile of serious medical texts on the table.

Liam shrugged. "As you can see, she laughed at the material. It's obviously not too difficult for her."

Ciaran smiled. "This is my brother, Tadgh. He's the new Sciphil Seven. Your home district."

Liam stepped back, nodding at Tadgh with the utmost respect. Ciaran chuckled on the inside as he saw Tadgh's face turn red. His little brother would never get used to formality.

Gaia had stopped laughing now and gazed at Ciaran and Tadgh. Then she flicked her glance back at Ciaran. "You look very pale, Ciaran. Are you sick?"

Ciaran winked at Gaia. "I see you're applying your medical knowledge already. What was so funny in these books?"

"You didn't answer my question, so that means my guess is right. You're injured."

"Gaia!" Liam warned.

Ciaran stopped smiling. It seemed as if Gaia had aged five years since he'd last seen her a few days ago. Her mental capacities were astounding. Even her tone of voice was different. But most noticeably, her innocent mind was gone. The child he had known was gone.

"I apologize. I must show you respect," Gaia said and hopped off the sofa. She reached out her hand.

"I assume you're after a handshake?" Ciaran narrowed his eyes.

"No. I'd like to fix your energy. I can draw from these lights. I have total control of that now. I won't touch any other part of the residence."

"Thank you, Gaia, but I think I can manage."

Gaia put on an almost royal smile and said, "As you wish."

Ciaran signaled Liam and Tadgh to step outside. "What happened in the last few days? She looks and sounds very different," Ciaran asked.

Liam ruffled his hair. "I don't know what to tell you. She's totally changed since we came here. It seems as if my Gaia has gone, and she's somebody else now. Sciphil Seven, is it possible for us to go back home?"

"I'm afraid that District Seven is unsafe right now," Tadgh said.

"I'm so sorry you're unhappy here, Liam," Ciaran said. "We'll try to get you home as soon as possible. Has anyone tried to contact Gaia here?"

Liam shoved his hands in his pockets and shook his head. He lowered his voice. "I saw her talking to herself once, though. It sounded like she was talking to someone, but I couldn't see anyone else. When I asked her about it, she brushed me off. She turned your household robot off once by sucking its energy out and pumping it into the garden. Then she drew from the light and turned the robot back on. When I asked her to stop, she said she needed to practice for the war that's coming. I know Eudaiz is at war, but she's only eight. She'd never even seen blood before she met you."

"What do you make of her ability to transport energy?" Ciaran asked.

"I didn't even know she could do it."

"May I ask how was she born?" Ciaran prodded.

"You mean, is she our real daughter? Yes, she's our daughter. She was born like any other child in Eudaiz."

"She was put in a box after she was conceived?" Tadgh asked.

Liam raised his voice. "Oh no! If you're implying that somebody replaced her when she was in the box, that's a horrible and cruel thing to suggest. Yes, my wife and I are ordinary Eudaizians, but that doesn't mean we can't have a child with special talents."

"That's not what we meant . . ." Ciaran said.

"Why are you arguing?" Gaia spoke from behind them, and Ciaran, Liam, and Tadgh jumped out of their skin. She stood at the entrance to the patio, looking somewhat distant. She smiled at Ciaran and stepped out into the garden. She stumbled on the steps, and Ciaran darted over, grabbing her before she fell face first onto the concrete.

And that was the last thing he remembered.

***

Zach strode quickly up the hill, followed by Dan. He saw the rainbows ahead. As Ayana had said, the rainbows marked the exit zone in the Daimon Gate. But these rainbows were different. His best friend, Dan, trailed behind, ruffling his sandy hair and muttering protests.

"Look, Dan, I've been through this route before. When I say it's fine, it's going to be fine."

"I'm telling you, this is weird."

"Bro, I know you're good at supernatural mazes and stuff, but this isn't supernatural—"

"I know it's the parallel universe you're talking about, but there have to be some fundamental rules of supernatural movements. It has to comply with astronomical arrangement and some other things I know you don't care for. I just don't think we should go up that hill."

"But the rainbows—I mean, the exit zone is up there!" Zach exclaimed.

"I'm not going up!" Dan said sternly.

"We are running bloody late! You don't know the implications of running late for a Sciphil officiation, but I sure do. In a nutshell, a lot of people will die if we don't show up on time!" Zach shouted.

"I am not going up that hill! If I have to die, I'm going to die down here. Not up there," Dan repeated.

CHAPTER 30

Ciaran opened his eyes to find himself lying in the garden bed, except he didn't recognize it now. Lawn, trees, flowers—anything he could classify as living was now dead and dried up. At one corner of the dead garden, Gaia sat, wailing. Huge tears rolled down her face. A few feet away from her stood Liam, looking helplessly at his daughter.

Tadgh crouched and helped Ciaran up. Liam was as white as a sheet.

"What happened?" Ciaran asked.

"It looked like she sucked the energy out of you—I don't know where she dumped it. And then she drew from the garden, as you can see, to put energy back into you. Then it seemed as if she was back to normal. She just flopped there and cried," Tadgh said.

"She won't let me touch her. She hissed at me!" Liam exclaimed.

Gaia sobbed louder, verbalizing something in Eudaizian.

"What did she say?" Ciaran asked.

"She thinks she made me mad, and she's sorry. She said she has things she needs to do, and she'll come back to me when she's finished," Liam said.

Ciaran looked at Gaia. He saw real tears. She was just a kid that had been thrown into a duty larger than life that she didn't understand. The words she had spoken to her father weren't hers. Ciaran knew this all too well. An innocent childhood cut short. An innocent mind robbed.

"I have some issues with my energy. There was a woman—I didn't see her, just heard her voice. She said I should come and see Gaia. Do you know who I'm talking about?" Ciaran asked Liam.

Liam shook his head. "I told you, she was acting strange and talking to herself in the last few days."

Ciaran approached and crouched beside her. "Gaia, may I hold you?"

The girl threw herself at Ciaran and sobbed. "She said I have to go with you. I have to help you protect Eudaiz."

Ciaran embraced the girl. "Don't worry, darling. You'll stay with your father. You don't have to go anywhere. Who is she? I'll talk to her."

"She's my mother," Gaia said, in tears.

"Your mother is dead, Gaia. She's no longer with us." Liam approached his daughter.

Gaia hissed and withdrew into Ciaran's arms. Liam backed away. "Father can take care of me if he agrees to let me be on duty. I need to help save Eudaiz." Gaia wiped her tears.

"Gaia, you might be a bit too young. But if you take a few more lessons from your father, I promise I'll put you on duty," Ciaran said.

Gaia smiled.

"Can I give you a hug now?" Liam asked.

Gaia nodded, slid out of Ciaran's arms, and ran to her father. Settled in his arms, she turned and spoke to Ciaran. "I drained your corrupted energy and put the natural energy back in. You should be fine now."

"Corrupted energy?"

"There was an artificial sort of energy that had been absorbed into every cell of your body. I don't know what it was or what it was for. But it was bad for you. So I took it away."

Ciaran nodded. "Thank you, Gaia. How do you know all that?"

"Mother told me."

Liam rolled his eyes.

"Can you tell me how to contact your mother?" Ciaran asked.

Gaia shook her head. "No, she doesn't want to see anyone except me."

Ciaran's wrist unit beeped, and he glanced at the message on the screen. It stated, "Dan's guest pass didn't work. He's facing Sciphil tests in the Daimon Gate. Need help NOW, or he'll die. Zach."

***

227

Their capsule descended into an ocean of smoke, fog, and white matter. The smoke was thick—so thick that Ciaran didn't feel safe landing the capsule by himself. He hovered the capsule and triggered the auto drive function on the control panel.

Tadgh sat in the corner of the capsule, saying nothing. Ciaran could tell his little brother was speechless out of fear whenever he was in the same vehicle with him, especially in an emergency situation. Tadgh had severe tachophobia—the fear of speed—a phobia that nothing in the multiverse could cure. On the contrary, Ciaran loved speed, and that didn't help the situation at the moment. Despite the attempt at robotic control, due to their momentum, the capsule landed violently and tilted to one side.

"Get out!" Ciaran shouted and grabbed Tadgh. They jumped out of the vehicle just before it exploded.

"That's the second vehicle we destroyed today," Tadgh muttered as he looked at what was left of the capsule.

"You should be glad you weren't in it when it exploded," Ciaran said and glanced around. The smoke was too thick for him to see much. "Remember the first test, Tadgh? This must be it."

Ciaran knew it wasn't possible for Tadgh to forget such an experience—the first test in the Daimon Gate. To qualify as Sciphil successors, they had to go through three stages of tests in the Daimon Gate. They weren't just tests—they were life and death battles in which the losers didn't just fail the tests, they were killed.

Without training and preparation, a person had a minimal chance of surviving the tests. Ciaran, Tadgh, Madeline, and Zach had passed them by the skin of their teeth. Of all of them, only Zach had had some preparation before traveling through the gate.

To avoid Dan going through the tests without training, Ciaran had arranged a guest pass that allowed him to go straight to Eudaiz without having to pass the tests. The reason the guest pass wasn't working was because someone in Eudaiz had altered the system and changed the records. Someone with skills, access to Eudaizian computer systems, and an intention to prevent the Sciphil Five replacement from being successful. The obvious person was either Kyle Wolf or whomever Kyle Wolf was working for.

"Over here!" Zach called out from the smoke.

Zach helped Dan walk out from behind a large rock. This was the first time Ciaran and Tadgh had met Dan. He was young, in his late twenties or early thirties, with sandy hair, even features, and extremely sharp green eyes. Zach said Dan had a wealth of knowledge and a natural sense for supernatural matter. He didn't have combat training or special physical abilities to fight the supernatural forces, but he somehow just understood how they worked.

Ciaran approached to give Zach a hand in taking Dan to higher ground where the smoke was less thick. Dan shook his head. "No, we should stay here. It's smoky, but it's kinda like the tail of the dragon. We should be fine here. We could run right into the eye of the dragon on higher ground."

"What the heck does that mean?" Tadgh asked.

"Is that the Japanese Zen maze?" Ciaran asked.

Dan nodded. "You know it?"

Ciaran shook his head. "I just know *of* it. So this stage is really designed to test you then, Dan."

"It's a physical round. You haven't entered it, and you looked like you've twisted your ankle already," Tadgh said.

"He told me it would be a walk in the park," Dan said and glanced at Zach.

Zach looked at Ciaran. "That's what I was told."

"Well, the test has opened. Can we reverse it or find another way?" Tadgh asked Ciaran.

"Please excuse us. A word, Tadgh," Ciaran said and signaled Tadgh to come with him.

From a distance, Zach and Dan could see Tadgh agitatedly raking his hands through his hair. "No," Tadgh said. Ciaran said something. "No, that's too dangerous!" Tadgh exclaimed again and looked as if he was going to stomp his feet. Ciaran said something further. "Fuck no!" Tadgh exclaimed again. But Ciaran seemed to have finished with their conversation, and he returned to where Zach and Dan stood. Tadgh followed, looking miserably grumpy.

"You've passed the tests, Dan," Ciaran said.

"What? But I haven't even entered yet," Dan said.

"That's all you need to know. I'll get you out of here. In one piece," Ciaran said.

Zach frowned, but said nothing. Ciaran turned on his heel. The group followed him in silence, each of them battling a stream of questions in their heads, which they didn't have the answers for. But there was one piece of information they all shared—one mistake inside the Daimon Gate would cost them their lives.

CHAPTER 31

A long while later, Ciaran, Tadgh, Zach, and Dan approached the exit zone of the Daimon Gate. Ciaran remembered it vividly from when they had passed the tests weeks ago. When Bran had tried to exit the gate after asking Ciaran to steal data from the EYE, the exit zone had been a dark dome with gothic arches and dimensional traps everywhere. Depending on the purpose of the passengers, the exits appeared at different locations and took different forms. Ciaran suspected that the EYE's sensor keyed in on emotional cues, reading whatever aura a passenger was emitting at that particular moment.

Now the exit looked like a peaceful rainbow, like it had never been used to kill anyone before and had never killed Bran right at this very spot. Contrary to the apparent peace, however, there were robotic scanners everywhere in the exit zone, continually capturing live data and utilizing the data fed from the EYE system to confirm the legitimacy of the passengers.

Ciaran shifted, feeling the disc in his pocket.

He took Dan, Zach, and Tadgh back to Lorcan's place. Lorcan was more than a computer genius who had helped him before, he was a friend. Ciaran used Lorcan's system to create fake data about Dan passing the tests. There was no other option. To create another guest pass, he would have had to go back to Eudaiz, and time didn't permit that. Ciaran placed the fake data and ensured that the information in the Daimon Gate system and in the EYE—the multiversal databank—settled.

During the whole process, Tadgh looked worse than if he was on a rollercoaster without a seatbelt.

The only thing Ciaran had to do now was retrieving the fake data from the Daimon Gate and inserting it into Eudaiz's system. He didn't risk putting it into his palm chip, the one that Bran had installed into his body. With a loose disc, he could always drop it if the system detected him and then deny ownership of it. Getting caught on his way out meant a death sentence. Even his father, the Host of Daimon Gate, wouldn't be able to help him then.

Ciaran verified at a control panel. A rumbling noise echoed as if an enormous door was sliding open. He needed only to pass through. When he got to Eudaiz, the Daimon Gate would not have the authority to stop him.

Tadgh narrowed his eyes. It wasn't the door to the exit zone that was sliding. Another dimension had opened, and an entrance to the Host's residence appeared. "Shit," Tadgh grumbled between his teeth, then grinned.

Their parents, Conan and Jennifer, came through the door. Conan frowned, but Jennifer was radiant and smiling. "There are my boys."

"Mother." Ciaran nodded and approached his mother for a kiss. Tadgh followed suit. Ciaran and

Tadgh shook Conan's hand. Then Ciaran turned and looked in the direction his father was frowning—there he saw the rainbow had turned into an imposing gothic dome, and he heard Zach gasp, "Holy shit!"

They all turned to look at Zach. He pointed at the dome. "Impressive," he said and manufactured a grin.

"How are my children, Mother?" Ciaran asked.

Jennifer chuckled. "Trying to be a good father now, are you?"

Ciaran smiled then gestured to Dan and Zach. "You know Zach from when he passed the Daimon Gate with me. And this is Daniel Chandler, the to-be Sciphil Five of Eudaiz. We're running late for his officiation, so I'm afraid we have to leave now."

Conan frowned. "A Sciphil? I don't recall a Sciphil test running through the system recently."

Jennifer glanced at Ciaran, then she turned to Conan. "Since when do you document every test running through all nine thousand gates?"

"We have nine thousand gates, but Eudaiz is the only participating universe that uses the

Sciphil system—and there are only nine Sciphil tests. I know when they're run." Conan stared firmly at Ciaran while answering Jennifer's query.

Ciaran stared directly back at his father. "I appointed Josephine Cassidy—Tadgh's girlfriend and your soon-to-be daughter in law—as Sciphil Four without her having to pass the Daimon Gate tests. You can't interfere with an affair outside the Daimon Gate, Father. But for your information, I'll be changing the process for future Sciphils. The Daimon Gate tests are not necessary."

"You can do whatever you want after your coronation, Ciaran. After you become king of Eudaiz. But now, under the old system, Sciphils going through the Daimon Gate for the first time must pass the tests unless there is a legitimate guest pass. Can I request your council for verification of Dan's position?"

Ciaran smiled. "Of course, Father. I'll be sure to sign off on the request when I get back to my tower." Ciaran felt a slight buzz from the device in his pocket. He nodded a goodbye to his parents and signaled Tadgh, Zach, and Dan to approach the exit.

"Ciaran," Conan called out before his son reached the scanning zone.

"Yes, Father."

Conan cleared his throat, and Ciaran could read the fear in his father's eyes. Although Conan wasn't his biological father, he was the only father Ciaran had known. He regretted causing him concern, but it couldn't be helped. If he walked through that scanning zone and the alarm rang, there would be nothing his father could do to save him.

"When will you return for your children?" Conan asked.

"As soon as I get everything in Eudaiz settled and complete my coronation. I have to go now, Father."

Jennifer saw Conan's reaction to Ciaran's approach of the scanning zone, and she called out, "Why don't you stay for tea, Ciaran?"

Ciaran turned, shaking his head. "I'm sorry, but I have to go, Mother." He felt the device in his pocket buzz a second time.

"You're not carrying anything out of here that you shouldn't be, are you?" Conan asked sternly.

"No," Ciaran said brusquely and turned on his heel. He slid his hand into his pocket and pressed a button to silence his device. Then he held his breath and walked through the wicked scanner.

Red lights flashed.

Alarm bells sang.

Conan's handheld device beeped its own alarm. He hurried to the control panel of the scanner. Ciaran flew at his father to stop him. Conan shrugged him off. "I have to turn the scanner off. I watched you die once. I can't do it again!" Conan cried.

Ciaran pulled his father away from the control panel which was flashing a red alarm. Conan slammed his handheld device to quiet it.

"Father, you can't cover for me like that. The machine caught me. The data is already in the system. There's no point in turning it off. But I haven't done anything wrong," Ciaran said.

The gate and the exit zone began to close. Jennifer pushed at Ciaran. "Go! Leave here!" A tear fell to her face.

"It's okay, Mother. I haven't done anything wrong," Ciaran said.

"Take your stubborn brother out of here, please," Jennifer called to Tadgh.

Tadgh approached Ciaran. Ciaran didn't move an inch. He stared at his father, and Conan stared back. "Can you honestly tell me you haven't done nothing wrong?" Conan asked.

"I have a disc with me, but I didn't steal your data."

"May I scan it?" Conan asked.

"For God's sake, let him go. Why would you want to scan his disc?" Jennifer asked.

"He triggered the alarm. It's protocol. If, as he said, he didn't do anything wrong, scanning the disc will only make things easier. If the disc contains no stolen data, then he's good to go."

Ciaran shook his head. "No, you may not scan my disc. It's my private property. But I guarantee that there is none of your data on it."

An officer in the Host's residence ran outside and called for Conan. "Sir! Alarm at gate 821 was triggered. The committee messaged you for a meeting."

"Well, this is gate thirteen, and the alarm of this gate is squealing, too. Ciaran, step out of the scanning zone, will you?" Conan snarled. It was rare for Ciaran to see his father lose his composure. Ciaran stood his ground, ignoring the alarm sounds from the scanner.

"The security at 821 was breached, and we've lost the subject, sir," the officer insisted.

"Step out of the scanning zone, Ciaran," Conan requested once again.

"I will, but I'll step to the other side of the gate. I'm not coming back in," Ciaran said, signaling Tadgh, Dan, and Zach to proceed. The group slid smoothly past the scanner and exited on the other side.

Jennifer entered the scanning zone.

"No, Mother. Please don't. I can handle this," Ciaran said.

"Do I have to call the guard on you, Ciaran?" Conan asked.

"Would you do that?" Ciaran stared at his father.

Conan stepped closer to the scanning zone. He stared back at his son, and then he shook his head.

"Sir!" the officer said.

"Shut up!" Conan shouted at the officer and moved to the control panel to turn off the alarm.

The officer gasped. Turning off the alarm to let the subject go before clearing him would violate the Gate's policy. Ciaran grabbed his father and spun him away from the control panel. Doing so caused Ciaran to step out of the scanning zone and back inside the Gate. As soon as he did so, the alarm stopped its screaming.

Silence.

Ciaran hesitated a moment. He looked at his father. "You may scan my disc if that helps clear any doubt," Ciaran said, removing the disc from his pocket and handing it to Conan.

"I know you don't want your information recorded in the EYE when I scan it, but you know our policies. No information here will be used to interfere with any matter outside the gate. I assure you that," Conan sympathized.

Ciaran nodded.

Conan slid the disc into a portable scanner. Shortly after, the screen flashed. A word appeared: SUNFLOWER. Conan stared at the word and then looked up at Ciaran.

"It's a flower," Ciaran said.

Conan removed the disc and gave it back to his son. He turned to the officer. "Now what were you talking about before?"

"The security at 821 was breached, and we've lost the subject, sir. The committee asked you for a meeting. I tried to message you, but your portable device was off."

Conan nodded. "I'll meet with the committee. What did we lose at gate 821?"

"I think we had a trespasser, sir. The system couldn't detect him, but it did pick up a portable device with data capability being transported out."

"We have no idea what kind of creature from which universe stole the data?"

The officer shook his head.

Conan nodded, dismissing the officer. He looked at Jennifer and could see her stress. He then turned to his son.

"I'm sorry," Ciaran said.

Conan swung his fist, punching Ciaran hard in the face. "Get out of my Gate." He turned and walked away.

Ciaran rubbed his face. He kissed his mother goodbye and strode through the door, heading toward Tadgh, Dan, and Zach. The alarm of the scanner sang again as he passed.

"You'll be in so much trouble next time you see him." Tadgh chuckled.

"At least—apart from my cheek—no one and nothing was hurt," Ciaran said.

"Except for your father's ego," Zach said.

Ciaran nodded. "I used him. I'm sorry for that."

"Your timing was impeccable, though. Wasting just enough time to get Nick past the other gate. How did you know your father would react to your tricking the alarm that way?" Dan asked.

Nick was a Xiilok man Ciaran had brought to the Daimon Gate before. He had been residing at Lorcan's place. In return for Nick's help in their previous trip, Ciaran had promised a placement for Nick in Eudaiz.

Ciaran smiled. "Blind luck."

Tadgh rolled his eyes and muttered, "Show off. Where's the disc now?"

"Still with me, of course," Ciaran said.

"What? So what did Nick carry through the gate?" Dan asked.

"A fake disc. Ciaran had two discs with him," Tadgh said.

Zach shook his head. "You brothers."

CHAPTER 32

Ciaran, Tadgh, Zach, and Dan stormed out of the transitional zone between the Daimon Gate and Eudaiz. The transitional zone was a no man's land. No landscape. No governance. And no lives. Ciaran was about to call for a capsule when a rail-free capsule approached and Sciphil Nine, Pete Chandler, jumped out.

Ciaran knew something awful was happening.

"Come on in!" Pete waved. After they had all rushed into the capsule, Pete punched the auto drive function.

"Situation, Pete?" Ciaran asked.

"Juliette is reforming. It started earlier than expected. It might be too late, but you have to be there at Tower Five. All available Sciphils are now in their towers to give assistance when you need it. But this won't be just an officiation. It will be a battle. If Juliette completes her reformation before you terminate her, don't come in. She'll kill you. Back away, and we'll shoot at Tower Five."

"How can you shoot at the tower?" Ciaran asked. "The nine towers are the pillars of Eudaiz. Without one, Eudaiz will collapse."

"We have no choice. That's what Ayana said to do. She's second in charge after you, and we weren't sure you'd come back in time."

"But I'm back now. And I'll go into Tower Five regardless. If Juliette has reformed, I will fight her."

"She'll be invincible, Ciaran."

"No one is invincible." Ciaran muttered and took control over the capsule. There was still a little bit of time left before they arrived at Tower Five. Ciaran looked at his wrist unit. He had been blocking Madeline's private communication channel. After the incident in the bed chamber, he couldn't bear to recall the look on her face. He couldn't stand the thought of what he had done. He rubbed his thumb across the surface of the panel then activated it.

On the small screen, Madeline's face appeared instantly. He didn't expect it to hurt so much to see her face. She had been waiting all day for him to turn this communication channel on. But now, she looked at him, saying nothing. He rubbed his thumb on the screen as if he could touch her face. This might be the last time they saw each other. He was going into Tower Five. Ayana must have briefed Madeline, and she knew the implications of his decision.

But she just looked at him now and said nothing. He didn't know what to say, either.

Juliette was his past. Madeline was his life now and his future. And now, there were children in their lives. But it might all end here very shortly.

The capsule dropped Ciaran and Dan in front of Tower Five. "Ayana has arranged guards, they will be here momentarily to guard the outside. I'll take Tadgh to Tower Seven. Zach, you come with me," Pete said.

"No, I'll stay right here. Outside the door. Even if you send troops, they'll need a leader," Tadgh said and hopped out of the capsule, not waiting for an agreement or disagreement from anyone.

"I'll stay here, too," Zach said and followed Tadgh.

Pete hovered the capsule a moment and then zoomed away.

***

Ciaran approached the gate of Tower Five with Tadgh and Zach flanking him. Dan stood behind. In front of them loomed the round structure of the gigantic Tower Five, intimidating to uninvited guests. Behind them, a group of two hundred guards arrived.

"Are you sure we need only two hundred?" Tadgh asked, glancing up at the tower that rose ominously to the sky.

"Two hundred non-robotic guards are all we can get at the moment," Ciaran said.

Ciaran turned on his the communicator in his wrist unit. "Everything ready, Sizx?"

"Affirmative," Sizx's voice reverberated from the speaker. "Tower One, are you in position?"

"Yes," Madeline said.

"Tower Two?" Sizx asked.

"Affirmative," Ayana responded.

Sizx repeated the process, receiving confirmation from Janei in Tower Six, Jo from Tower Four, and Pete in Tower Nine.

Ciaran tucked the machine away. "Ready?" he asked Dan. Dan nodded.

They approached the Tower Five entrance. Ciaran verified himself on the control panel. Nine round layers of concrete and steel shuddered and spun, lining up to reveal a walkway to the inside. Ciaran looked at the walkway, realizing that if even a single layer changed its mind and swung inward, they would be ground like pepper.

The layers closed up behind them as they moved through. He smiled. So far, so good. The dome of the central chamber opened up in front of them.

The officiation chamber was colder than others that Ciaran had been to. Or maybe it was just his imagination. It had been a while since he had seen Juliette—the haunting ghost from his past. Regardless of what they had done to each other, the simple truth was that there had once been love between them.

In the middle of the room was a massive glowing glass chamber. Juliette stood inside, her eyes half-open. Her hair was flaming red, and her face gained radiance as every second ticked by.

Ciaran said to Dan, "I'm sure Zach has explained the process to you. But I need to repeat this—Juliette won't be able to get out to do any harm to you. You see the cone-shaped stone on the ceiling of the glass chamber? That's her keystone. At the moment, it's supplying her with her eudqi. Once she reforms, she'll be invincible. I'm going to disconnect her keystone at the control panel here, and that will kill her. After that, you'll enter the chamber, and I'll reconnect the keystone. You will then receive the eudqi of Tower Five and officially become Sciphil Five. Everything clear?"

Dan nodded. Suddenly, it felt as though the building were shifting. The nine layers of the outside walls started spinning.

"Is that part of the process?" Dan asked, concerned.

Ciaran shook his head. "Someone unauthorized is trying to get in."

Ciaran looked up. Juliette's eyes were fully open now, peering down at him. Ciaran instructed Dan to remain in his position and then charged to the control panel. He verified himself and entered the keystone command. A beam of light streamed from the wall and flashed straight into Ciaran's face. He staggered and stumbled. The floor under his feet slid open, and he dropped down. Dan charged over and attempted to grab Ciaran's arm, but he ended up falling down the hole after him.

CHAPTER 33

Outside Tower Five, Tadgh yelled into the communicator. "Why are the walls spinning? Something's happening inside. Let me in!"

"Possible intruders identified. I can't get signals from Ciaran. He authorized you as second in charge, Ayana. What's your command?" Sizx asked.

"What do you see around you, Tadgh?" Ayana asked.

"Not a thing. But it's like an earthquake in here."

"You don't see anyone? No creatures around the tower? Can you confirm?"

"No creatures. I sent men around the tower to check. They saw nothing. Now the nine gigantic walls are spinning like crazy. Is the tower going to cave in?"

"Tadgh, Kyle is inside," Madeline chimed in, her voice as cold as steel and her face as white as a sheet. Tadgh spewed a stream of profanity, and Zach stood still, saying nothing.

***

From a basement inside the tower, Ciaran scrambled up and tried to get his bearings. He heard Dan stomping around in search of a door.

"The light blinded me. What do you see, Dan?"

"I think we're in a basement—or maybe a tunnel."

"You're right, Dan," Kyle's voice echoed from a dark corner.

Ciaran reached for his gun but found out he had lost it during the fall. He pulled out his dagger but knew it was useless because he couldn't see a thing.

"How many of them?" Ciaran asked Dan.

"Six."

"You can only smuggle in half a dozen Black Rock creatures at a time. Do you really think that's enough to take over Eudaiz, Kyle?" Ciaran asked.

"I certainly do." Kyle chuckled.

Ciaran felt the impact of a black beam, and blood gushed out from his left shoulder. He heard Kyle growl, communicating in a strange language. It sounded to him like Kyle wasn't happy that his man had shot Ciaran.

"I don't need five men to kill you now," Kyle threatened. Ciaran heard the men rushing at Dan. He could hear him fighting and then grunting, maybe because he'd been hit. Ciaran felt the impact of Kyle's foot on his abdomen. The kick sent him staggering and flailing backward.

He could see a dim light. He knew he was regaining his sight, but it was going to take time, and at the moment, the vision wasn't enough for him to fight Kyle effectively. As Ciaran stood up,

Kyle kicked him again. Ciaran fell to the floor, rolling. Kyle approached and stomped his foot down on him. He grabbed Kyle's ankle when he felt the impact and flipped him down to the floor.

Kyle roared in rage. He pulled Ciaran up, threw him against the wall, and pressed his sword to Ciaran's throat. Ciaran couldn't see much, but he could hear Kyle's men pounding on Dan in the background. He tilted his head aside to avoid the blade and used all of his strength to land a firm kick on Kyle. Kyle fell backward, bellowing.

Dan had been captured by three creatures. He grunted and shoved at them, but didn't seem to be able to free himself.

"Stop, or they'll kill him!" Kyle shouted. Ciaran had been charging in Kyle's general direction, but he stopped in his tracks when he heard his threat. Kyle kicked him again, and then pinned him to the wall, his sword at his throat once again.

"You underestimate me, you arrogant prick." Kyle pressed the sword harder. "I swear I could cut your throat right now and taste your blood. But that's too easy. Too painless. I want you to live to see the end of Eudaiz and to watch what

I'm going to do to your lovely wife and your children."

"You won't live to see me suffer through that." Ciaran pressed hard against the sword. Thirty percent of his vision had now returned.

Suddenly the tower shook as if shuddering under the impact of a new power. Kyle grinned. "My timing is impeccable. I'm afraid I'll have to let you live a little longer, Ciaran. Juliette has reformed. Don't you owe it to Eudaiz to terminate her? A note of warning, though—she can be quite a bitch." Kyle punched at piece of stone on the nearby wall with his finger, and a set of stairs leading back up to the ground floor slid out from the wall.

"Thank you, Master," Kyle whispered.

"Who's your master?" Ciaran asked, earning another hard kick from Kyle. Kyle picked Ciaran up and held the sword against his throat from behind.

"I have shaky hands, Ciaran. You wouldn't want me to slip." He pushed Ciaran up the stairs. "Take Dan up," Kyle commanded his creatures. They crowded Dan and pushed him up the stairs after Kyle and Ciaran.

On the ground level, Juliette had completed her reformation but hadn't yet exited the glass chamber. It had been a lifetime since Ciaran had seen Juliette truly alive. She looked at him with the innocent eyes he had fallen in love with the first time they'd met at Oxford University.

"Juliette! Well and alive. A magnificent creature!" Kyle muttered.

Juliette smiled. "Kyle. Sinful and ugly. A condemned creature!"

Kyle laughed, and his sword cut into Ciaran's neck slightly, producing a stream of blood. Juliette frowned at the sight of it.

"We need to talk, Juliette, or you'll see more blood from him. Just for your information, he's still human. Losing too much blood will not be good for him."

"I have nothing to talk to you about!" Juliette said.

"Oh, you do, darling. You were built to take the first sacrifice to get the Silver Blood for the Master. All I need you to do is to tweak things a little bit. Make it my name instead of his."

"I don't work for you," Juliette snarled.

"I am not asking you to work for me. Just make that little change, and I'll let your husband live."

"He's no longer my husband." Juliette stared straight into Ciaran's eyes, which had regained one hundred percent vision. What he saw in her eyes was loss—the loss he had seen years ago just before she died in his arms.

Kyle said nothing but pressed the sword harder against Ciaran's throat.

"No, don't. All right!" Juliette cried.

"You're no longer my wife, Juliette. You and I owe nothing to each other. You don't have to do what he says," Ciaran said and earned another stream of blood as Kyle deepened the cut of the sword.

***

Outside the tower, Tadgh shouted into his communicator, "Can you hear what Madeline just said? Kyle's inside with God knows how many men. I'm outside with two hundred fucking guards. Let me in. Stop the spinning walls and let me in."

"Your command, Ayana," Sizx's voice came across.

"My tower's gate is spinning. I'm under attack," Sciphil Nine, Pete Chandler said.

"Same here," Janei Chartel, Sciphil Six, added.

"My walls are spinning, too. Tell me how to stop them," Madeline said.

"Why are all the walls in all of the towers spinning?" Tadgh asked.

"Ayana, I know you're under attack, too. What's your decision?" Sizx asked.

"All active towers are under attack at the moment. You all have to stay put and guard your tower. I'll help Tower Five. The officiation inside makes it the most vulnerable target."

"If you just let me inside Tower Five, I can help Ciaran," Tadgh said.

"I'll stop the spinning walls of Tower Five to let you in, Tadgh. Sizx, send my power from Tower Two to Tower Five," Ayana said.

"That will leave you unguarded, Ayana." Pete's voice shouted from the speaker. "I'll do it! I can fight them off. Sizx, send my power to Tower Five."

"Ayana's in charge, Pete," Sizx said.

"I'll stop my walls!" Pete shouted.

"I won't allow that, Pete," Ayana said.

"Send mine. I'll stop my walls," Madeline said.

"You don't have the authority or the experience to do that. You'll get all of your people killed. Stay inside. Sizx, send mine," Ayana said.

"Copy," Sizx said.

CHAPTER 34

Inside Tower Five, Kyle had pushed Ciaran against a wall, prevented Juliette from leaving the glass chamber, and forced her to change control of the Silver Blood to him. Juliette's eyes remained locked on Ciaran's the whole time. Ciaran knew she wouldn't give in easily. That was her personality. It was a trait he loved. But he wasn't sure how long she'd be able to hold on.

Kyle grew more and more agitated. If he killed Ciaran, Juliette wouldn't give him what he wanted. If he didn't, then he still wouldn't get it. Ciaran ran through various solutions in his head, but all of them would require Juliette's cooperation. Now more than ever, he appreciated Madeline's psychic ability. He wasn't a psychic, but because their minds, hearts, and soul were connected, they were able to communicate at critical moments—moments like this.

Did that mean he and Juliette had really never connected?

Dan wriggled hard but couldn't get out of the grip of the two gigantic creatures holding him. He said, "Silver Blood is a negative source of energy drawn from female qi at the right astronomical moment. It has to be done in harmony with the ying and yang elements as well. If you do it incorrectly, if you force her to do it now, you will waste years of preparation."

"What are you talking about?" Kyle roared.

"I'm saying you're doing it wrong. And you are about to waste years of accumulated energy," Dan continued.

"Bullshit!" Kyle blustered and turned toward Dan. Taking the opportunity, Ciaran hit the hilt of the sword, knocking it from Kyle's grip. Ciaran swiveled, lowered himself to the ground, and swiped Kyle off his feet. He followed with several hard kicks, and Kyle rolled across the hard floor like a soccer ball.

Kyle's creatures were distracted and unsure what to do, and Dan broke free from them and ran. Kyle stood up and howled in anger. He stretched his arms out, and then his body. He was transforming from a normal human shape into something more wolflike. Ciaran grabbed Kyle's sword and slashed at him. It felt as if the sword had hit a wall of solid steel.

The Black Rock creatures had caught up with Dan and reached for him. Juliette whirled out of her glass chamber and darted in Dan's direction. From behind, with one swing of her arm, she sliced all three creatures in half. Their bodies dropped to the floor and evaporated into thin air.

Kyle had finished his transformation. He'd completely turned into a monstrous half-man half-wolf creature and stood tall on two legs, teeth bared. The sword Ciaran had was useless against him. Kyle grabbed Ciaran by the neck and threw him into the wall. As he scrambled up, Juliette ran over to stand next to him. They stood side by side, just as they had during their marriage, confronting all the challenges life hurled at them.

Kyle howled again and charged at them both. Juliette swung her arm again, but just as with Ciaran's sword, her blade did no damage. Kyle flew at Juliette and snapped his teeth at her shoulder. Ciaran swung her out of the way, and Kyle's teeth scraped his shoulder. Juliette fell to the floor. Kyle charged at Ciaran. Ciaran put all the strength he had into a kick at Kyle's face. Kyle staggered back, shrieking in fury.

***

As soon as Sizx transferred the power from Tower Two to Tower Five, the nine gigantic walls of Tower Five stopped spinning. They lined up, revealing the entrance. "You have one tenth of a slot before the tower begins to spin again," Sizx warned. Tadgh grabbed his daggers and guns. He didn't know how long one tenth of a slot was, but he guessed he should move quickly. Zach checked his own weapons. He shifted the gun Ayana gave him to make sure it was in place.

"Ten of you, come with me." Tadgh waved. The guards charged in with him.

The walls started to spin again immediately after Tadgh, Zach, and the men passed through. They darted into the hall and saw the fight in progress.

Kyle fought solo now as all of his creatures were dead. Dan was on the floor, conscious but bleeding. Ciaran looked injured, but he moved around with Juliette, who was bleeding but still looked quite agile. Kyle whirled around, growled, and grumbled some unintelligible words. He sought an opportunity to attack Ciaran and Juliette, but as they had their backs together, encircling Dan, Kyle couldn't figure out the best approach.

Ciaran saw Tadgh and Zach enter the hall with the guards, he smiled at Kyle. "I'm afraid it's your time to die, Kyle."

"I'm invincible! See if you can slash at me," Kyle tried to roar, but the sound came out like a howl.

"Your pathetic tricks give you a steel body. But you still have a soft head, Kyle," Juliette said.

"And weak brain power," Ciaran muttered.

Kyle screamed. "What I don't have, no one can have. Keep the Silver Blood for your Master.

Without Eudaiz, see what he can do with it!" Kyle ran to the glass chamber.

"No!" Juliette shouted and hurried after him. In the chamber, Kyle threw his black sword at the cone-shaped keystone affixed to the ceiling. Juliette flew over, using her body to block the sword from damaging to the stone. At the same time, she turned her right arm into a steel blade and brought it down, slicing from the front to the back of Kyle's head. Her body was pinned to the stone. Kyle convulsed, collapsed, and died. His body melted into a pool of black liquid and evaporated into the air.

Juliette's body fell to the floor like a pile of bloody clothes. Ciaran knew she had no chance of surviving the impact, regardless what people had said about her being invincible. The keystone was everything to a Sciphil. She'd die to protect it. And yet, he was here to terminate her.

Ciaran ran to the chamber. Juliette reached up her hand and slammed it on the control panel. The door swung closed right in front of Ciaran.

She leaned at the glass panel, putting her hands on the glass. "Will you forgive me for what I've done, Ciaran?"

"I have one question, Juliette—was anything between us real?

"You hurt me with that question, Ciaran." Tears rolled down her face.

"You hurt me with everything you've done," he said.

She stared at him for a moment, then she said, "Without knowing my answer, will you still forgive me because I was your wife?"

He looked at her—blood smeared her beautiful face and tangled her magnificent red hair. Those innocent eyes were still so striking. They looked at him, waiting for his answer. He nodded. "I forgive you, Juliette."

She smiled. "Then I'll pay you back. Remember, Ciaran, I was your wife, and I loved you. I don't make excuses for my actions. I served the Master. I'm truly sorry to have caused you pain." She turned around and approached the control panel. Ciaran hurried to the outside panel, but it wasn't responding to his commands.

Inside the glass chamber, Juliette placed her palm to the panel. It activated and flashed a strange red light Ciaran had never seen before.

"Who's your Master?" Ciaran asked.

Juliette shook her head. "Keeping his secrets is the least I can do for him now."

The computer spoke in monotone voice, "Silver Blood processes activated. Please make your statement."

"What's that? Dan, you talked about Silver Blood before. What is it?" Ciaran shouted.

"I have no idea. I just bluffed to buy some time with Kyle," Dan said.

"It's the source of super power . . . so . . . she is the first sacrifice for the Silver Blood," Zach whispered, eyes wide.

"What the heck does that mean? Will she destroy this tower?" Tadgh asked.

Ciaran punched the glass panel of the chamber. "Juliette, get out here!" he commanded.

Juliette said, "Being your wife was the only time I actually got to live and be myself, Ciaran. My love for you was the only real thing in our marriage. Everything else was a plot. Thank you for giving me those precious moments." Ignoring Ciaran and his cries for her to get out, she turned toward the machine and said, "I, Juliette Dubois,

Sciphil Five of Eudaiz, commit myself, my energy, my source of power, and my soul to the creation of Silver Blood. The power will be directed to Sciphil Three—the king Sciphil position—and the appointed guardian of the Silver Blood is," she turned and looked at Ciaran, "Ciaran LeBlanc."

As soon as she finished her statement, her body exploded into millions of red light particles. They whirled inside the chamber and spun like a tornado. The chamber shook violently. Then a portion the red particles came together to form a shiny silver liquid and funneled upward, streaming into the keystone. When the particles and liquid had streamed into the keystone and vanished, the chamber stood empty as if nothing had ever happened inside.

The tower shuddered and shook a bit. Everyone crouched, waiting for an explosion. Nothing came. The tower returned to its imposing quietness. The chamber door swung open, and a line of text appeared on the computer screen. "Attention Ciaran LeBlanc: Sciphil Five position is empty. You have two days to fill the position."

"We have him ready now. How's that for being efficient!" Tadgh muttered.

Zach and Ciaran were still staring at the empty chamber. Suddenly, Zach gasped, "The stone observer said there were two sacrifices for the Silver Blood. The second one will be Ayana. Shit!" He turned on his heel and ran.

CHAPTER 35

After arranging for Tadgh and Dan to stay behind to guard Tower Five, Ciaran took Zach to Tower Two to assist Ayana. In the distance, thick black smoke streamed from Tower Two to the sky. The smell of burned flesh and electrical fire engulfed the air. Ciaran squinted his eyes as he viewed the scene through the monocular. He turned on his communicator. "Sizx, how many guards did you deploy from central to Tower Two?"

"Four hundred, as you commanded. Do you want me to send more? I'm not sure about the current status. They destroyed the data sensors over there."

"Do you know if their protective shields are operational?"

"In theory, yes. I only used the power of Tower Two for one tenth of a slot to stop the spinning walls at Tower Five, just long enough to send Tadgh and his men inside. After that, Tower Two regained complete power. But I don't know how many Black Rock creatures have slipped inside while their security was down during that one tenth of a slot."

"Can we get in now?" Zach asked agitatedly.

"Patience, Zach. We have nine towers to take care of, and we can't afford to have a single one down," Ciaran scolded. "Sizx, give me the status of the other towers."

After a moment, Sizx came back online. "All other towers report the attacks have stopped and their protective shields have stopped spinning. Casualties are minimal. All casualties from our side have been central guards. No casualties or injuries reported from Sciphils."

That meant Madeline in Tower One was safe. Ciaran drew in a breath and felt relieved. He knew it was selfish of him to think about her at this critical moment, but he couldn't help it. He was human, and she was his family. He spoke into his communicator, "The peace might be a decoy, a trick. All Sciphils are to remain in their towers until I say otherwise."

"Yes, Ciaran," Sizx responded.

Ciaran signaled Zach to approach Tower Two. When they closed the distance, they saw a sea of Black Rock creatures outside. The smoke and the smell of blood was from their guards—Eudaizian were made of flesh and blood, just like humans. They moved toward whatever was left of the four hundred central guards Sizx had sent. They were surrounding the tower from a distance, unsure what to do next since their previous attempt to attack the Black Rock army had obviously failed.

Ciaran approached three commanders who were still alive. Sizx had sent four—one for each one hundred soldiers. Judging by the way soldiers were standing around, Ciaran wagered the guards weren't as nearly as skillful and tactical as they should be. There were about three hundred left now. Their sheer numbers should help, but they needed strategy and structure to be effective.

After Ciaran sketched out quick instructions on tactical movements, the guards charged at the line of Black Rock creatures surrounding Tower Two.

Ciaran reckoned it was only by luck that they had taken down nearly five hundred creatures and hadn't appeared to lose many on their side. The Black Rock army didn't put up much of a defense. It was almost as if they expected to be slaughtered. Bodies and body parts scattered the field as Ciaran and his men fought through the enemy.

This was too easy to be true, Ciaran thought as he approached the gate and verified himself. The walls stopped spinning, revealing the entrance. Zach followed close behind. Ciaran signaled for him to take ten guards inside.

The stench of blood and gore permeated the air inside. The dead bodies of the Tower Two guards littered the floor. Ciaran heard the faint sound of a fight from the central chamber.

"They're going for the keystone. Stay right behind me, Zach," he whispered and signaled his troops to move in that direction.

Zach grunted a response and veered in the direction of another wing, despite Ciaran's cursing.

The creatures attacking the central chamber were combat trained in one-on-one fight. They had put down a number of Ciaran's men at the front. Ciaran noticed the creatures were not tactical—they had no battle strategies. He instructed his troops to follow his simple strategy. A small group fought in the front and quickly retreated. The Black Rock creatures were duped into chasing them, and then the rest of Ciaran's troops surrounded them in another hall and easily slaughtered them.

The number of creatures inside was more than he expected. There had to be at least thirty of them. By the time Ciaran had cleared the hall, there were no guards left alive.

It was finally quiet. Zach approached from another direction, a fresh wound bleeding on his arm. "I got them all at the other corner."

"If you refuse to follow my commands, I'll send you out right now, Zach," Ciaran warned.

Zach raised his arms, making peace. "All right, all right. I will."

Several bloodcurdling screams came from the main chamber. They echoed along the long steel corridor and bounced and distorted so much that

Ciaran couldn't tell whether the scream was from his guards or from the Black Rock creatures. Ciaran and Zach charged toward the keystone chamber—it was locked.

CHAPTER 36

Ciaran verified himself at the lock control panel. The steel door hummed for a second and slid open. Inside, Ayana sat by herself next to her keystone glass chamber. There wasn't much life left in her. Her body was battered, her clothes were covered in blood, and her magnificent white hair was tangled and dulled with bloodstains. Her beautiful blue eyes had turned gray and were glazed and lifeless.

Zach darted toward Ayana and crouched next to her. "Oh Jesus Christ, I'm so sorry Ayana. I should have been here. I should have fought with you."

She smiled at Zach. "No Zach, you were on an important mission. This isn't your fault. I'll recover. Don't worry." Then she looked at Ciaran. "I knew you'd come. I knew you'd save the tower. I'd never let go of my keystone, Ciaran."

"Of course not. You're a true warrior, Ayana. Let me take you inside the glass chamber. The energy from your keystone will heal you." Ciaran crouched to lift Ayana up.

"How are the other towers?" Ayana asked.

"They're fine now. Your tower seems to be the only one in trouble at the moment," Ciaran said.

Ayanna gestured for Ciaran to stop taking her to the glass chamber. "I don't want the chamber running until I'm sure all of our uninvited guests are outside the tower."

"I think we've cleared them. Is that right, Zach?"

Zach nodded and didn't say anything further. He scanned the chamber to check that no creatures had gotten inside. "I fought something . . . someone . . . out in the main hall, Ciaran. He wasn't an ordinary soldier. Not a creature . . . not even human . . ." Ayana said.

Ciaran pulled out two guns, holding one in each hand.

Ayana shook her head. "Guns won't work. He didn't have a shape. When he attacked, the force came at me like steel. Like thousands of steel blades. But when I returned the hit, my weapons hit thin air. Guns, swords, daggers—everything went through him without causing any damage."

"If he's invisible, how do you know he's not in here?" Zach asked.

"He's not invisible. I saw him when the beams from my gun bounced off the steel panel and the light reflected on him . . ." She paused to catch her breath.

Ciaran added, "He can de-materialize himself when he wants? This is more dangerous than being invisible. But still, he couldn't penetrate reflective light. So he does have weaknesses."

Ayana nodded. "Reflective light is one of his weaknesses. But I don't know what the others might be. I activated the light shield when I got in here. I think it's been keeping him out of this chamber."

Ciaran nodded. "You're doing really well, Ayana. The light shield is made of light beams that reflect back and forth between steel panels. If our theory that he can't penetrate reflective light is correct, then he wouldn't be in here. But we still have to go out there and clean him up, whoever he is. We can't be caged in here forever. And you have to get into that glass chamber to heal."

"We don't know how to kill him," Ayana said.

"As long as he has weaknesses, I'll find out what they are, and I'll kill him. No one is invincible, Ayana," Ciaran said, recalling Ayana's comment about Juliette being invincible after she reformed.

"I'm sorry you had to terminate Juliette. Regardless of what happened between you two, you've shared your life with her once," Ayana said and paused to catch a breath.

Ciaran said, "I didn't terminate her. She terminated herself after making a statement about her dedication toward the Silver Blood and naming me guardian."

"Did she?" Ayana muttered.

"I don't know anything about Silver Blood. But Zach said you would be the second sacrifice. Sciphil sacrifice isn't an acceptable term in my realm. You're my councillor. I demand that you discuss everything with me first before doing anything drastic regarding Silver Blood. Do I have your promise?"

"I—"

"I've got him!" Zach shouted. Zach stood in the middle of the chamber, holding his temples in his hands and concentrating. As a sound bender, he could send sound waves into anyone's head if he could locate the person. "I hit randomly in the room outside, and I think I've got him."

They couldn't see anything through the closed steel door. Ciaran turned on the monitor but didn't expect to see much since the man appeared to have no form that the computer could capture. "We have to get out there, Zach. If you can locate him with your sound waves, hit him hard. As soon as he makes a noise, I'll head in that direction."

"Sounds like a good plan. Let's go kick that prick's ass," Zach said.

"Weapons can't harm him, Ciaran," Ayana reminded him.

"No ordinary weapon can, Ayana. But I'm not planning to use ordinary weapons on him. We'll be back shortly to heal you in the chamber. Can you hang on and wait for us?" Ciaran asked.

Ayana nodded, and closed her eyes, resting. Ciaran nodded at the door, signaling Zach to head out of the room. As soon as the door swung open, they stormed outside.

CHAPTER 37

The long hallway of Tower Two which connected to the main hall was cold and empty—the kind of emptiness that occurred when the energy was sucked out of it. The bodies of guards were scattered over the floor. The Black Rock creatures' bodies had evaporated. The ceilings in the hall were almost transparent, and they let in some of the fading light of dusk. It was growing deeper into the night, and Ciaran knew his body was going to shut down soon.

The man or the creature they meant to hunt was nowhere to be found.

Zach concentrated and glanced around. Ciaran knew he was sending his sound waves randomly, scanning the area. Ciaran hated to admit it, but he had experienced those sound waves before, and it wasn't pleasant. Zach could hit a frequency that was shattering to the ear.

If the man intended to ambush them, he wouldn't be able to get close. Ciaran was sure Zach was scanning a wide perimeter of the grand hall to protect them both.

Suddenly they heard a grunt. Zach turned in the direction of the sound and sent more sound waves. There was a flashing light. A man's shape appeared, turning red and blue under the impact of the hit.

With one thought, Ciaran could send out a blade of fury—his personal weapon that no creature could handle. He called it a blade, but he could actually mold it into the form of a sharp-edged weapon of any size and degree of power. But Zach was in range. The only way Zach wouldn't be hit by Ciaran's blade was if he stood next to Ciaran.

"Over here, Zach!" Ciaran called out.

Zach was concentrating and didn't hear Ciaran. The position Ciaran was in was ideal for sending out his blade—he was in a corner with his back to a wall. From there, he could wipe the entire hall out with one hit and cut the man into thousands of pieces. Ciaran left his position and moved closer to Zach, who stood in the middle of the room next to a column.

But before he could send out his blade, Zach grunted, and blood trickled from his mouth. Ciaran knew the man had struck back. Zach's sound bending bounced back at him twice as hard when he encountered a strong opponent. This immaterialized man might not be a strong opponent, but he appeared to have found a way to strike back at Zach.

Zach sent another wave, but it bounced back to him so hard that it sent him straight to the floor. As Zach was scrambling back up to his feet, Ciaran sent the blade of fury straight toward where he had just seen the flashing lights and the man's shape.

Ciaran knew he had missed. Something as hard as steel hit him, sending him crashing to the floor. Blood gushed from his right shoulder. It felt like he'd been stabbed. Ciaran was about to jump back up, but an idea crossed his mind. He slowed down and pretended to have been hurt more than he was. He sat up slowly.

There, he felt it. A pressure in the air—something moving toward him. Ciaran held his blade in his mind like a bow and shot it out toward where he guessed the man was. He reeled the blade in slightly so that it didn't fan out and hit Zach.

Ciaran's blade hit the man. He bellowed in pain. It sounded more like an animal's roar than a human cry. The shape of a man glowed brightly, flashing blue and red. The blade hadn't cut the man into pieces as Ciaran had hoped, but it had certainly caused damage. In the glowing shape, Ciaran saw a face—it was oddly familiar. He'd seen this face before. The face vanished quickly before Ciaran could figure out whom he was seeing.

Feeling the pressure in the air coming at him again, Ciaran sent his blade toward it. He heard a thudding sound as if a body had dropped to the floor. Ciaran sat up, looking around. It seemed as if the man had suffered a hard hit and had run away.

Suddenly, it came at Ciaran like a storm. He wasn't sure he would be able to block it because he couldn't see where it was. Zach darted toward him and shot continuous sound waves in that direction. The man turned red and blue again. Then it was as if things occurred in slow motion. Ciaran could see the collision coming, and could anticipate the consequences, but he could do nothing about it.

The man turned toward Zach and reached out an arm which had turned into a sword. He still couldn't see the man's face, but he saw the steel blade in its most prominent material form as it pierced Zach's chest from the front to the back.

CHAPTER 38

Ayana stormed through the corridor. She could no longer wait for Ciaran and Zach to return. The strange voice of a man chanting in her head was getting stronger by the second. It was calling her to sacrifice for the Silver Blood. Was it Bran talking to her from his grave?

But Bran didn't have a grave. He was a Sciphil, and he had died like a Eudaizian. She couldn't even find his stone. When he died and giving his energy to Ciaran, she wasn't there to see where his soul had gone. She had lost him forever. She hadn't seen him for more than thirty-three years.

But that absence was much less painful than the fact that he'd died right after their reunion.

At least for thirty-three years, she'd lived with hope—the slim chance that she would be able to see him one more time, hear his voice one more time, and feel the aura of a great leader from him one more time. The slim chance to find out if he had ever thought of her as someone more than just his protégé.

Now, she was sure he was gone forever. So why had he come back with that strange voice?

Juliette had made the first sacrifice, naming Ciaran as guardian. So it had to be Bran who wanted it. Bran was calling for her to finish it off, to take the one in a thousand opportunity to create such a power for Eudaiz.

But something wasn't right. Something in the voice told her it wasn't Bran who was speaking to her.

She heard it again, urging her to make the statement. She needed to find Ciaran and Zach. The voice pounded in her head. "Yes, I'll do it for you, Bran. You only have to ask," she whispered, staggering her way through the corridor, tracing her hand along the wall to keep her balance.

"Good girl. Enter the chamber. Make your statement. I'll tell you who to name as guardian . . ." the voice chanted.

Her world stopped in a skidding halt. "You're not Bran. Who do you want me to name as guardian?" she asked. The grand hall opened in front of her, and she saw Zach lying in a pool of his own blood and Ciaran pushed into a corner by something invisible. Steel swords flew at Ciaran from all dimensions. He couldn't fight back because the opponent was nowhere to be seen. Ciaran just blocked what blows he could.

Ayana ignored the voice in her head and charged into the hall.

The sound of her entering the hall stopped the flying swords for just a second. Seizing the moment, Ciaran crouched and once again screamed out his blade of fury. Ayana knew that this killing machine was Ciaran's talent. It came like a tornado with spinning steel blades, and it could gut a universe if he so chose. Ciaran usually pulled it back to avoid collateral damage. But this time, it didn't look as if he was holding back. The blade hit a barely visible shape in the middle of the room, and the voice in Ayana's head vanished, replaced by a man's cry.

In front of them, the distorted shape of a man appeared, flickering. There were brief flashes of eyes, of a face. It was so fast they couldn't recognize the person, but they could tell the he had suffered horribly. Then the image vanished again, and they could tell he had fled the hall. There were blood trails on the ground. They could hear the echoing growls of pain and then sound of the tower's steel door grumbling.

Ciaran ran to Zach, who was gasping for air. His head rested at an awkward angle, and Ayana lifted it. His beautiful green eyes were glassy, and blood trickled from a corner of his mouth. She had never had a son, but now she understood what it felt like to lose one.

"We'll take you to the chamber. We'll fix you. Don't you die on us, Zach, do you hear me?" Ciaran asked.

Zach looked at Ciaran. "Mya . . ." he whispered.

"What?" Ciaran said.

"Her name is Mya Portman. She helped me recruit Dan for you. She saves . . . she saves lives .

. . She violated the rules of her world to save me . . . I left her in the Daimon Gate . . . I promised I'd come . . . back . . ."

"Listen, Zach, if you promised a woman you'd come back for her, then you will." Ciaran hauled him up, trying to get him to the keystone chamber. But Ayana knew that Zach's human life was finished.

CHAPTER 39

Ciaran put Zach down next to the chamber. He was barely breathing and was no longer responsive to anything Ciaran said.

"What are you doing, Ciaran?" Ayana asked.

"I'm taking him in. The chamber will heal him."

Ayana shook her head. "That only works in normal situations. This wound is fatal. And the eudqi will only heal him if he's a Sciphil."

Ciaran realized now why Bran had to sacrifice himself to save him. His injury in the Daimon Gate had been a fatal one. Bran had had no choice but to appoint him as Sciphil Three. He had shoved him into the chamber to absorb the eudqi, realizing that his own injury was fatal and that giving the Sciphil position to Ciaran meant he wouldn't be able to be healed by the Sciphil eudqi.

"You want to appoint him as Sciphil now so he can be healed by the eudqi?" Ciaran asked.

"Yes, but I'm not the one appointing him. You are. And we haven't much time."

"Where are you going?"

"Nowhere. I'll be nowhere and . . . nothing."

"No . . . you're not doing what Juliette did, sacrificing for the Silver Blood or whatever it is."

"It's the dream of any king of Eudaiz, Ciaran. Bran would have wanted it for you."

"I'm not king yet, and it's certainly not my dream. Now if you'll excuse me, I'll take Zach into the chamber."

Ayana shoved her way into the chamber and punched the control panel to shut the door on Ciaran.

"I don't need Silver Blood. I need you to be my councillor. Please come out," Ciaran growled.

Ayana smiled. "You're a good man, Ciaran. Bran would be proud of you."

Ciaran looked at the woman inside the glass chamber and saw someone desperately in love with his biological father. She would do anything for him, and she looked for nothing in return. As Ayana bent over, bracing her hands on the control panel to regain her balance, Ciaran saw a necklace spill out of her top. A bare chain.

"You used to wear that necklet with a charm, didn't you?" Ciaran asked.

Ayana touched the chain and nodded. "A locket my mother gave me before she passed away. I've lost the charm."

Ciaran stated firmly, "No, you didn't. Bran had it. When I met him in the oblivion hole of the Daimon Gate, he had that locket in his chamber. When we left, he took nothing with him but that. He wouldn't let me touch it, and he wouldn't say what it was. For the thirty-three years he lived in the oblivion hole, that locket was the only connection he had with you. And he held on for that long because of you."

Tears rolled down Ayana's face.

"He loves you, Ayana. It's hard for a man in his position to admit to it. But he has loved you the whole time."

Ciaran had never seen Ayana so happy. Tears of joy flowed from her eyes. "Thank you, Ciaran," she said and then returned to the control panel. She placed her palm on the verificator, and Ciaran saw the surreal red light he had seen when Juliette made her statement. Ayana said, "I, Ayana Dee, Sciphil Two of Eudaiz, commit myself, my energy, my source of power, and my soul to the creation of Silver Blood. The power will be directed to Sciphil Three—the king Sciphil position—and the named guardian of the Silver Blood is Ciaran LeBlanc."

As soon as she finished her statement, she vanished, disintegrating into the tornado of red and silver substance inside the chamber. The chamber shook, the room shuddered, and the entire tower vibrated. For a long moment, Ciaran thought the whole universe was going to collapse. But it didn't. Everything soon returned to its normal imposing quietness.

Ciaran then carried Zach into the glass chamber and performed the procedure to appoint him as Sciphil Two. Shortly, Zach returned in his enhanced form—a rightful Sciphil Two. Ciaran looked at Zach and knew Ayana would have been proud.

CHAPTER 40

Ciaran strode into his bed chamber—a walk he took every night. But tonight, it seemed like an eternity. Part of him wanted to rush in and pull his wife into his arms, but the other part wanted to return to his control room and work . . . or hide. He didn't know how many times today he'd thought he would die and never get to see her again. Two important women had died today for an elusive source of power that he didn't care about. He dare not imagine if one of those women had been Madeline. He wouldn't know what to do or how he would continue in this universe if that had happened.

Would anything he was doing making any sense?

His mind constantly reminded him of how violent he had been with her the night before. He couldn't bear the thought that he had hurt her. It could have been so much worse. Would he ever be able to touch her again in the same way?

In the bed chamber, Madeline was waiting. She had changed into her sleeping gown. The room was in the same condition as it had been when they'd left it in the morning—mostly trashed.

Ciaran didn't rush over to embrace her. Instead, he hurried to the bathroom to wash his face and stood staring into the mirror, unsure of what to do next. She entered the bathroom and held him from behind.

"I—"

She cut in and said, "If you're going to say you're sorry for what happened last night, your apology is not accepted. I told you—it wasn't you. I know what it was."

"You kn—"

"I haven't finished. If you want to apologize for shutting me out, apology is still not accepted because that isn't enough. I don't take it lightly when you have a problem, and you choose to lock me away and go about handling it yourself." She held his hand and led him out into the bedroom.

He looked into her beautiful brown eyes and knew he could drown in them at any moment. He brushed his thumb over the dimple on her left cheek, his ingrained habit. "I'm sorry," he said.

"Not enough, Ciaran."

He nodded. "I know it will never be enough. We need to talk."

She pushed at his chest so he fell into a reading chair, the only chair left upright and intact in the chamber. Then she came and sat on his lap. "Then talk." She twirled her fingers into his long, dark hair.

"I broke my promises to Bran. After all we've been through with Juliette, after all she's done, I still forgave her for what she did."

"She was an important part of your life. If you didn't forgive her, that resentment would follow you your whole life. It's not worth it. And your forgiveness turned out well, didn't it? She took the first sacrifice for the Silver Blood."

"You know all about the Silver Blood?"

"No, not until I went to see Moira. The antidote she gave you the other day contained traces of Silver Blood. But only a simulation, not the real thing. Moira told me Silver Blood has been in the cosmos for thousands of years. To create it for Eudaiz, they needed two sacrifices from female Sciphils. All female Sciphils were told they would have a chance to sacrifice for the greater cause. I didn't know about it because you officiated me, and grandfather didn't have a chance to talk to me about anything before he died."

"We don't need a source of energy like that. I can create super soldiers and any kind of weapons we need to defend Eudaiz. It will just take some time."

Madeleine chuckled. "Oh, you'll want this Silver Blood! Trust me. It's a super source of energy absorbed from the cosmos. You told me the way our ceilings are designed in such a way that it maximizes our ability to absorb the best sources of energy at all times. But that's because we can't control the energy of the cosmos. Silver Blood is totally controllable. You can create, store, and distribute it. And once it's inside a body, you can actually turn it on and off."

"If it's such a good source of energy, wouldn't you want it on all the time?" Ciaran asked. Then he answered his own question. "I guess everything comes at a cost. The energy must have a catch so that you wouldn't want it on all the time. But apart from controllability, what is that about Silver Blood that needs such sacrifices?"

"Its ability to heal. Moira told me it heals all injuries as long as the person hasn't died. It's pretty handy, I think." Madeline smiled.

Ciaran nodded. "Invincibility. The power of super soldiers."

"Yep. And you are now the guardian of it. Of course, you won't have a hand on it until after your coronation."

Ciaran rolled his eyes. Madeline hopped up and kissed his left eyebrow. "Face it. Someone has to do the king job. It can't be that bad."

"Before Ayana died, I told her Bran had loved her his whole life. I saw the locket that he took and held onto for the entire thirty-three years he lived in the oblivion."

"That's very sweet. She loved him with everything she had in her. It's good to know he loved her, too," Madeline said and kissed his right eyebrow. Then she paused. "Wait. You're telling me this because you lied to her?"

Ciaran closed his eyes and nodded. "I lied to a dying woman when she took the sacrifice to give me the power."

"She didn't give you the power, she gave it to Eudaiz. And the only reason she did so was because she thought Bran wanted her to. You never know—maybe he loved her for real."

"No, I wouldn't know."

She pressed him down, sinking into the chair with him and kissing him.

"Madeline, I . . . I don't . . ."

"Don't want to hurt me again? Try me." She kissed his neck and worked her way down his chest. Ciaran put his hands loosely around her waist. She jerked her head up and looked at him. "Ciaran, do I need to tell you how to do this?"

"I . . ."

She reached up and yanked his shirt open, then she violently ripped it off his body in one swift move. The sound of the tearing fabric intrigued him. She grabbed her gown and tore it off. She wore nothing underneath.

Ciaran swallowed hard. His hands ached to make a move. His pulse raced. His blood began to boil inside his veins.

Madeline reached for the buckle of his belt, and before he knew it, she had yanked the belt off. She grabbed his hands, rubbed them against her smooth skin. Up and down. Slowly. Up and down. His hands always knew exactly the right places to roam. But now they felt useless, heavy, lost. They needed her guidance to travel over those dips and curves. He needed to rediscover those corners of her body and soul, her secret places of pleasure that only he knew.

His body tensed, but she drove him with hips that had already given them their twins. She bent down and ravished his lips.

There. His brain exploded. He kicked over the last lamp they had left in the bedroom and sent the room into complete darkness. Their bodies tangled, and they rolled from the chair to the floor with her on top. He flipped her over and pleasured her in every way he could possibly think of—if his brain could actually think at that moment.

More sounds of torn fabric—it could have been the tablecloth. She kicked a table leg and might have broken it. The table collapsed onto one side, and all objects on it fell to the floor.

They rolled elsewhere and continued their physical exercises. After a long while, they lay spent next to each other in heaps of sweat, their bodies still tangled, trying to catch their breath.

"Sometime, say, in the next millennium, you might have to roll off me so I can breathe, Ciaran."

Ciaran rolled off and planted a kiss on her temple. "Better?"

"Hummm..."

He kissed her lips. "Better?" he asked.

"That's good."

"I can do better. But we should probably get decent as our robot will most likely storm in here at any time for the routine report. I haven't yet had a chance to reprogram him."

Madeline lay lazily on the floor, wrapping her leg over Ciaran so he couldn't get up. "I know what Robert's going to say. He'll say your coronation is next week. In the next few days, there will be truckloads of activity over at Sciphil central. We're going to have to settle all the Sciphils and prepare billions of civilians for the celebration of your coronation. And make sure security is at one hundred percent capacity."

"Since when do you do Robert's job?"

"If you don't want him in here, then I will have to give his little report."

The green light at the top of their bed chamber door flashed four times.

"At least he's learning how to knock on the door—in his own way," Ciaran said and sat up, expecting the robot to come in. Madeline pulled him down to the floor again.

The light on top of the door began to flash orange.

"What does that orange light mean?" Ciaran asked.

"That means the door is jammed, and the robot can't get in." Madeline grinned.

Ciaran laughed. "You've learned how to use the machine jammer! I underestimated you, First Councillor."

Madeline kissed his cheek and bit his bottom lip lightly. "My king, I jammed the door using my shoes."

END OF MINDSCAPE TWO

MINDSCAPE THREE

PART ONE

DEAD SQUARES

CHAPTER 1

Jo spat the black liquid she'd thought was coffee back into the mug and put the mug back on the console of her control station. The dim light from the sky dome seeped through the semi-transparent ceiling and reflected on the polished floor and the shiny computer monitors on the wall. She normally preferred monitors to wallpaper, but at the moment, it seemed a little too much for her. She'd been staring at the monitors for so long that her eyes felt like they were bleeding.

She needed some caffeine to jolt her system. She had to catch up on her research for the job at hand—being Sciphil Four—a position that made her responsible for more than a hundred billion civilians in her district.

Jo considered herself a good computer designer. On Earth, as the Steel Princess, she was unbeatable in the hologame community. She had only ever lost to Ciaran, who played as White Knight. That was good enough for her when it came to computer games. She wasn't nearly as good as Ciaran in computer programming, but that was only because he had more resources than she did.

She clucked her tongue to herself. In the hologame and in matrixes, being able to see patterns was a crucial skill. She was definitely as good as he in recognizing patterns. Ciaran was good because he had a wealth of knowledge about...well, about almost everything. But he had the unfair advantage of being conceived in the Red Stage of the Daimon Gate. And from what Jo had heard, children conceived there were considered to be the best beings in the cosmos.

Her parents were bakers and lived in New York. They had a modest cake shop in town that had earned them enough money to put her through college. But her ability to see patterns hadn't come through education. It was her natural talent—or maybe her curse. Because of that so-called talent, she'd ended up here—in this strange universe where none of her life experiences or skills applied.

She missed her coffee and the bagels from her brother's bakery. For the life of her, she couldn't get her robot to make a decent cup of coffee. She missed hanging out with her best friend, Madeline, and watching silly chick flicks. And she missed the time she had been Tadgh-free.

"Ted!" she growled as she leaned down to her computer keyboard and banged her head against it a few times. Sometimes her robot's name sounded much too close to Tadgh.

"Yes, Jo!" Her home robot rolled in. He was as round as a soccer ball and stood at knee height. Although he had working limbs, he usually chose to roll instead of walking.

"I gave you the precise recipe for coffee, yet you brought me this disgusting black liquid! How hard can it be to make a cup of coffee? If you show me where the ingredients are, I'll make it myself. Is there a coffee shop in town? There has to be one."

"I make the coffee according to your formula. However, some of the organic ingredients you gave me aren't available in Eudaiz, so I took the liberty of using some substitutes."

"Well, that's the problem. Coffee isn't simply black liquid with caffeine. But taste is something I doubt you'll ever understand."

"I am afraid that human tastes and preferences are too complicated to program into a home robot like me."

"I'm sure Ciaran's Robert has the correct program!"

"Robert isn't just a home robot, he's the first generation of—"

"All right. I get it. No need to elaborate, Ted." Then she sighed. "I'm sorry. I'm a little testy—"

"Obviously!" Tadgh's voice interrupted. Without invitation, he sauntered in and began to massage Jo's shoulders.

"Why wasn't Tadgh's arrival announced?" Jo asked Ted.

"It was." Ted pointed to the door monitor. There she saw the blinking message that Tadgh had just arrived at her residence. She had been testing a program that would allow her friends in without scanning. Apparently, the system considered Tadgh to be her friend.

"So what are you testy about, Sciphil Four?" Tadgh asked. "Nothing I did, I hope."

She shook her head. "I can't put my finger on some programs."

"Anything I can help with?" Ted asked.

Jo arched an eyebrow. "What kind of analyses can you run?"

"I don't have the ability to conduct any analytical processes. But I do have access to data. I can gather the data for you using any data retrieval algorithm you wish. The speed of my—"

Jo raised her hand to stop the robot. "You're saying I can dictate search commands to you, and you'll pull the data for me? I don't have to deal with this monstrous search engine with its odd search terms and algorithms?" Jo's voice had increased noticeably in pitch, and she shifted in her chair to gather her composure. She removed Tadgh's hands from her shoulders so that he stopped massaging them.

Tadgh pulled up a chair and sat down next to Jo. She cleared her throat and lowered her voice. "Now, Ciaran's coronation will be next week. I imagine it'll be a huge event in Eudaiz, and there will be many badasses in the cosmos lurking around to try to ruin the day. I'm assuming security will be strict, but I want to see if there's any potential danger the ordinary system might have missed."

"Affirmative," Ted said.

"Ciaran wouldn't want his coronation ruined, so I suppose Tower Three is already secured. But have the security risks of the other eight towers been assessed?"

"Yes. In order from the most to least secured— Tower One, Tower Seven, Tower Nine, Tower Two, Tower Six, Tower Five, Tower Eight and Tower Four."

Jo nodded then frowned at Tadgh's expression. "What's wrong?" she asked.

"You're the most unsecured Sciphil during the coronation," Tadgh said.

She frowned again and recalled Ted's report. Tadgh was right. The robot had said Tower Four was the least secure. "How can I rank even lower than Sciphil Eight, the guy we haven't even met?"

"Sciphil Eight has been on a mission and will return by coronation time. He has no record of a security breach in the last fifty years," Ted said.

"On what basis does security rank me as most risky?" Jo asked.

"The security committee has twelve members. The head of the committee, Sizx, Eudaiz's head of intelligence, has developed a..."

"Who? The blue-haired chick? Oh, come on! Give me a break!" Jo exclaimed and pushed up off her chair.

Tadgh pulled her into his arms. "Calm down, darling." Then he turned toward Ted. "What are the criteria for security ranking?"

"History of Sciphil succession. Origin of the current Sciphil. And security records," Ted answered.

"All right. What's the succession history of the Sciphil Four position?" Jo asked and sat down on Tadgh's lap.

"Hoyt Flanagan. Tor Linii. Manix Lunn. Bly Srico. Kyle Wolf. And you, Josephine Cassidy."

"Well, I know I'm human. Kyle Wolf is Eudaizian. How many other humans are in the successor line?"

"Hoyt Flanagan and you are both human. The rest were Eudaizian."

"Okay, so what's the succession line of, say, the Sciphil Three position?" Tadgh asked.

"Pierre LeBlanc. Aedan LeBlanc. Ealga LeBlanc. Malachi LeBlanc. Bran LeBlanc. And the current king-to-be, Ciaran LeBlanc."

Jo turned around and saw Tadgh looking at her. There was one thing that Tadgh and Jo had in common—they were both good at recognizing patterns. And Tadgh was brilliant at numbers. He could even calculate the probability of pattern occurrence in his head.

Now, they both saw a pattern emerging.

"Apart from Sciphil Three, are other Sciphil positions running within a family?" Jo asked.

"It has been the case in the past. But the latest generation of Sciphils has changed. Sciphil Two, Zach Flynn, has no blood relation to Ayana Dee. Daniel Chandler has no blood relation to Juliette Dubois. He does, however, have a family tie with

Sciphil Nine, Pete Chandler. And with you, Tadgh."

Tadgh nodded. "As Sciphil Seven, I have no family tie with Ralph Durant. But I do have a blood tie with Ciaran."

Jo nodded and said, "So the Sciphil Four line of succession is a mumbo jumbo."

"I was wondering why Hoyt Flanagan didn't appoint a human successor for the Sciphil Four position," Tadgh said. "And why other Eudaizian Sciphils didn't appoint their relations. They have family ties in Eudaiz, like we humans.

Jo stood up and paced back and forth. "When Kyle kidnapped me on Earth, he had an entire army working for him," she said. She turned and looked at Tadgh. "Wait a second. All Sciphil Fours before me didn't have blood ties. They were all Eudaizian...born from boxes. I want their birth records, Ted."

"Unfortunately, you don't have access to that information."

"Ahhh... so who does?" Jo snarled.

"Ciaran," Tadgh said before the robot could reply.

"All right," Jo muttered and engaged her computer system to create a holocast to Ciaran's residence. "District Four. Tower Four. Me—Sciphil Four. Now there are four Eudaizians in this line of Sciphil succession," she said.

Tadgh nodded. "Yes, there's a pattern. But of what? What would make a pattern of four? Four gods? Four elements? Like metal, water, fire, and earth?"

She chuckled. "Or simply the four points of a square. But all of these Eudaizian Sciphils are dead now. So that makes them dead squares."

The computer monitor blinked a couple of times, and then the screen went blank.

"What the hell?" Jo looked at the monitor.

"Look out!" Tadgh shouted and dove at her. He hit her so hard they both fell to the floor.

In front of them, the computer exploded.

CHAPTER 2

Madeline stormed into the control room and saw that Ciaran had just finished giving instructions to staff and had programmed a couple of bug-like robots. He raised a hand to gesture her to wait. Once the staff had cleared the room, he turned toward her.

"Jo and Tadgh are fine." He approached her and rubbed his thumb on the dimple on her left cheek.

Madeline exhaled, releasing a ton of anxiety. Her psychic ability had decided to balk when she'd needed it the most. Ciaran kissed her. He always did that—before she could rant, ask questions, or complain about anything. The next thing she knew, she'd almost forgotten what she had stormed in here for.

"Fine? As in not dead? Free from injuries?"

He smiled. "Jo and Tadgh were thrown into a dimensional hole as a result of the explosion. But Jo managed to shoot a message back here before the hole closed. The message said they were both okay. She'll get back to us when she can locate their physical position."

"Are you sure she can?"

He nodded. "I am. And they're free from injury—that's the most important thing. I can't say the same about Jo's robot, however."

Madeline narrowed her eyes. "Wait...how did Jo's home robot get to your control room?"

"I picked him up and transported him here."

"You've been to Sciphil Four's residence and back?"

He nodded and smiled. "I'm efficient."

Madeline sighed and said nothing. She was busy asking their own home robot, Robert, to teach her to use the inter-universal communicator so that she could call the Daimon Gate directly to check on the children.

He rubbed his thumb on her chin. "I have something to discuss with you, First Councillor."

Damn it! Her hormones were always stirred up whenever he called her First Councillor. Maybe it was because of the way he said it. Maybe his British accent was what turned her on. She cleared her throat. "Sure."

He smiled again. "Promise me you won't get upset."

She narrowed her eyes. "Jo was really injured?"

He shook his head.

"Tadgh?"

He shook his head again.

"You?"

"Promise me!"

"Okay, I promise."

He nodded. "I was able to retrieve the last search function Jo performed on the robot before the explosion. And the information—or rather, what I can deduce from it—warranted some attention."

She paced the room. Her psychic feelings started to creep in, none of them good.

Ciaran grabbed her shoulders, holding her still. He looked into her eyes. "Jo thinks someone related to the succession line of the Sciphil Four position is planning to do something catastrophic before—or maybe on—the day of my coronation. And it has something to do with Dead Squares because when she said the words, her computer system exploded."

When it came to computers, Madeline didn't need to ask Ciaran or Jo whether they were sure about their speculations. They were usually right, at least most of the time. She sighed and nodded.

Ciaran continued, "It could be anything. It could be a chess move...or a location. Jo thinks it might have something to do with the way children are born in Eudaiz. I've checked the profiles of all four Eudaizian Sciphils. All were born in District Four. And I don't think the profiles stored in the system are authentic."

"So what's the part you think I'd be upset about?"

He sighed. "I'm afraid it could get a bit more complicated. I think it has to do with the number four. Considering the four Eudaizian Sciphils, Kyle Wolf was number four. That was why he was so ambitious. He wanted to be king of Eudaiz."

"And that's why he ended up dead," she said.

Ciaran nodded. "Because Kyle wasn't meant to be king. Whoever planned the ennead codes either wants to be king or wants to build the rightful king for Eudaiz. Judging by how someone tried to pry information out of my mind and the way we were attacked before, I think it has something to do with children born in the Red Stage of the Daimon Gate."

"So it might have something to do with you and our children," Madeline said.

"Three of us, and maybe one more," Ciaran said. "If what Moira claimed is true—that she had a daughter conceived during the Red Stage of the Daimon Gate, and her daughter is alive in Xiilok, her daughter is number four."

"So you think it might have something to do with Moira?"

Ciaran nodded. "And that's the upsetting part for you. I know you sympathize with her situation. And given she's my ancestor, I should be more sympathetic. But I think that not only does Moira want to build super soldiers to find her daughter, she also wants her daughter in the king Sciphil position." He turned and looked into her eyes. "You know I don't care whether I'm king or not. But I'm a firm believer of nurture over nature. If Moira's daughter was raised in Xiilok—the land of the multiversal outlaws—and was brought up by her captor, a traitor of Eudaiz, then she's not fit to be the queen of Eudaiz."

"Ciaran."

"Yes, First Councillor."

This time, his First Councillor sounded cold. He spoke it almost like a reminder that she held a position with great responsibilities, and all personal matters and feelings must be set aside. "What do you want me to do, Ciaran?"

"Break your promise with Moira. We will not help her find her daughter."

She stared at Ciaran. "You remember that our children were born using Moira's technology. You can prevent her from having direct contact with the children, but there's nothing to stop her from remotely controlling the birth chamber."

"You don't have to tell her anything before we have a chance to secure our children."

"Let me get this straight. You want me to not only break my promise with that poor woman but also lie to her. Okay. Fine and dandy. I'll do that for the sake of my children. But when push comes to shove, when Moira needs an answer, I will not upset her."

"I told you we can secure the children. And they're *our* children by the way."

"No, Ciaran. If you could have taken our children out of those boxes—before they hatched—you would have done so already. So as long as our children's lives are in Moira's hands, I refuse to upset her."

"Our children aren't chickens. They don't hatch. And I told you I would get them out of those boxes," Ciaran growled. "Be patient. Make yourself unavailable to Moira. That way, she won't ask you questions, and you don't have to lie. That is, if you insist on holding your moral ground with her."

She snarled back, "I know you have a universe on your shoulders, and I realize you take your responsibility seriously. Unlike a petulant councillor like me."

"That's not what I said."

"It's what you implied. Keep your moral ground, and stay up there on your high horse. Take care of your universe. But I am a mother. My children will always be my top priority. They are not yet safe and sound in my arms, so there is nothing you can say or do that will change my mind. Do your best, and keep Moira away from me." She strode out of the room, breaking her promise to him.

She was royally upset.

CHAPTER 3

The cold breeze seeped up from the ground and absorbed into her fragile skin. Jo shuddered. She couldn't tell whether she was still in Eudaiz or had been transported into another dimension. But she didn't care for the eeriness around her at the moment. It reminded her of her darkest days in New York—the ones she didn't care to remember and had never told anyone about, including her best friend, Madeline.

She glanced around. Tadgh was nowhere to be found. She didn't have Madeline's psychic abilities, but she had a feeling he was alive and looking for her.

He was her second chance in life, and she wasn't about to take their relationship for granted. She promised herself when she found him that she would make more of an effort to make their relationship easier. She couldn't keep letting her past haunt the most beautiful thing happening in her in life.

From the corner of her eye, she saw the shape of something moving in the dark.

"Who's that?" she shouted and reached her hand out for her gun only to discover she didn't have it. *Damn it*, she cursed silently. Because she had been working with a computer in her control room before being plunged down into this dark hole, she hadn't had any weapons with her. She hadn't been prepared.

The shadow grew larger and wriggled toward her.

"Don't come near me. I'll hurt you!" she shouted again, having no idea yet how she intended to hurt a ten-foot-tall, human-shaped shadow. The air around her thickened, and the space seemed to close in on her. The ground lifted up and lowered as if it was breathing, and a small amount of liquid oozed out on the surface from seemingly nowhere. It seemed as if the air around her had liquified and materialized, acting as a curtain that the shadow was pushing against.

Jo turned around to run. It was the most sensible solution given the circumstances. Her face smashed into a jelly-like wall, and she felt her head bounce backward. She squinted and saw a light that seemed to come from her right-hand side, via something that shaped like the entrance to a cave. The entrance was closing. She wasn't in a hole—she was in a cave. The air smelled awful. The shadow in front of her became more prominent and seemed to be coming closer. The good part was that it was getting smaller as it closed in.

Jo realized it had looked gigantic before because of the distance and the light distortion. The ground beneath her rose and fell, rose and fell.

The shadow came right up to the jelly-like wall and was separated from her by only the thin layer of a damp tissue. It clawed and pushed at the curtain as if trying to find its way out—or in.

Jo glanced again at the closing mouth of the cave. It was time for her to flee. As soon as she turned, she heard the shadow calling her name.

"What the hell? Who's that?" she asked.

The sharp tip of an object poked at the gelatinous curtain from the other side, and a dagger slipped through, slicing it open. The curtain parted to reveal Madeline, covered in a slimy substance. Jo heard moaning from somewhere deep inside the cave. Hot, putrid air pumped out in waves.

"Madeline!" Jo exclaimed.

Madeline looked at the rising and falling ground where Jo was standing and tried to maintain her balance. She glanced to the far end of the cave on her left and then to the closing cave mouth on her right.

"Is this place alive?" Madeline asked.

Jo realized that Madeline might be right. It looked like they were in the mouth of a living creature, and it felt as if the creature was either going to spit them out or swallow them. Personally, she preferred the former.

For a limited time, D.N. Leo gives away
4 books in the Multiverse Collection

CLAIM YOUR FREE E-BOOKS
http://narrativeland.com

THANK YOU FOR READING!
D.N. LEO

D.N. LEO 'S NOVELS
SERIES READING ORDER

http://www.narrativeland.com/dnleo-series-reading-order

—

A SHADE OF MIND
(narrativeland.com/shade)
Main Characters: Ciaran, Madeline, Tadgh, and Jo
(Recommended reading in order)
1-4 Random Psychic
2-4 Forever Mortal
3-4 Elusive Beings
4-4 Imperfect Divine

—

SPECTRUM
(narrativeland.com/spectrum)
Main characters: Lorcan, Orla, Roy and Mori
(Recommended reading in order)
1-4 White Curse
2-4 Blue Fox
3-4 Indigo Stone
4-4 Red Moon

—

MINDSCAPE
(narrativeland.com/mind)
Main characters:
Ciaran, Madeline, Tadgh, Jo, Kyle, Hoyt, Ayana, Pete, Sizx, Lorcan, Orla
(Recommended reading in order within series, can be read in ANY order in related to other series)

Queen's Gambit
Knight & Pawn
Lone Castle
Doubled Bishops
Dead Squares
King's Endgame

—

SILVER BLOOD
Main characters:
(narrativeland.com/silver)
Ciaran, Madeline, Tadgh, Jo, Caedmon, Sedna, Roy, Mori, Zach, Mya, Lorcan and Orla
This series can be read in ANY order within the series and in related to other series.

Virgo
Libra
Scorpio
Taurus
Pisces
Gemini

Thank you for reading.

If you enjoyed reading **Mindscape Two**, I would appreciate it if you would help others enjoy this book, too.

Recommend it. Please help other readers find this book by recommending it to friends, readers' groups and discussion boards.

Review it. Please tell other readers why you liked this book by reviewing it wherever you purchase the book from. If you do write a review, please send me an email at info@dnleo.com so I can thank you with a personal email.

COPYRIGHT

MINDSCAPE TWO

By D.N. Leo